The Mullah
with No Legs
and Other Stories

ARI B. SILETZ

INTERCULTURAL PRESS

For information, contact:
Intercultural Press, Inc.
P.O. Box 700
Yarmouth, Maine 04096, USA

Book design by Jacques Chazaud
Cover design by LetterSpace
Printed in the United States of America

97 96 95 94 93 92   1 2 3 4 5 6

Library of Congress Cataloging-in-Publication Data

Siletz, Ari B., (Ari Barkeshli), 1953–
    The Mullah with no legs and other stories / Ari B. Siletz.
        p.   cm.
    ISBN 1-877864-10-2
    1. Iranian Americans—Fiction.   2. Iran—Fiction.   I. Title.
PS3569.I4215M85   1992
813'.54—dc20
                                                    92-1366
                                                    CIP

To mountain path

Contents

v

Introduction

The amazing patchwork of sounds and rules we call language contains clues as to the distant ties of nations. As a young student learning English, I was puzzled and vaguely delighted to note occasional similarities in words and grammar between English and Farsi. Why do these strange and remarkable people say "star" in almost the same way we do? Why do we form our comparatives in similar ways? I did not know it then, but in those similarities I was hearing the kinship between long separated members of the same tribe—a linguistic "Hello, cousin" from across hundreds of generations. A long time ago, we can only guess when and where, my ancestors and the ancestors of the people that now say "star" sat with their children by the same fires and told stories of even remoter pasts. The stories in this book are told with this tribal kinship at heart. It is true, we do not live in the same village anymore, and our languages and cultures have gone their separate ways, but for the duration of these stories, let us pretend that we have been separated for only a short time and that the storyteller is offering us a way to catch up on each other.

Much of what we have heard about Iran in the last decade has dealt with explosions and executions. There has been a war. Families have been destroyed and life has been wasted. The newspapers tell us about strife and fanaticism in Iran. These reports are true, but the types of stories we hear about a nation determine our attitudes toward her people. There are other stories from Iran, equally true, that do not paint the country in dust and blood. The version of Iran I offer here acknowledges the recent violence, but its focus is not on current events. These are episodes from the lives of my friends and relatives who do not habitually take hostages or demonstrate in the streets. Instead, their opinions and actions are handcrafted from parts of their day-to-day lives. The anecdotes emphasize growing up, loving our children, catching cold, buying bread, fearing death, and growing old.

As I remember these people, I also see their gardens and their poetry. I see the patterns on their silverware, the decorations on their doors, the lilt of their music, and the forest of Persian carpets on which they live. In depicting a culturally authentic Iran, it was natural to invite these rhythms to influence the style of the writing so that I would remain loyal to the idioms of Persian storytelling. Each story in this book is influenced by a different type of Persian carpet. In this way, the storyteller hopes to weave his plot in metaphorical identification with the most traditional and intimate of Iranian crafts. As a result, where events form a natural focus, there is a climax and an ending; where life does not sort itself into a hierarchy, each moment is allowed to stand on its own.

The style, intent, and content of these stories seek to deliver an antidote to the Associated Press rendition of Iran. On the other hand, turbulence in the Middle East has been so persistent that political upheaval has been stirred right into the traditions. An honest overview of modern Iranian culture will inevitably encounter a major source of that upheaval: the overwhelming influence of Western culture and technology. So, in the course of reading about everyday life in Iran, the reader will gather a grass-roots understanding of Iran's relations with the West from what the characters say, think, and do.

Introduction

To avoid the easy militancy that sometimes accompanies the literary treatment of people in conflict, I have taken a multicultural approach. I have drawn as much on my long stay in the United States as on my Iranian past. This has been easy, since my kinship with Americans is not limited to prehistory: I have two children who are Americans. They trace their ancestry to Iran, Turkey, Germany, and Scotland. They are happy and intelligent children whose playfulness celebrates the reunion of a scattered humanity. I cannot guess in what part of the world they will settle when they grow up, what languages they will speak, or what nationalities they will marry into. Our children are powerful reminders of our multicultural futures. They give us a personal reason to have concern for the future of all cultures. In relating these tales, my loyalties lie with Iran, the land where I was born and where my ancestors are buried. But my loyalties also lie here, in California, where my children were born and will be raised. I am also devoted to the rest of the world, where our descendants will mix and match with little regard to the colors of our flags.

We have arrived at an age where our voices and images carry across the planet riding on beams of light. Today, the touch of the remotest human is no further away than tomorrow, and as nations draw closer, so do their weapons and their wastes. Try as we may, how much longer can we maintain the illusion of separateness? It is time to believe that humans are, once again, one community. The bonds of compassion that held us together as a tribe are calling to be reestablished so they can hold us together as a world.

The Lions

In the summer before I started second grade, my father was given a new post in his government job. His first duty in this position was to visit all the branches of his office across the country and compile a report. This was a formidable task made easier by a few consolations: he was allowed to take his family with him, the visits would be short, and the report would not be read. On the other hand, the branches were numerous and the roads were brutal. Even the journey between two major cities, such as Shiraz and Ahwaz, had to be endured on an unpaved, unmaintained, and dangerous road.

• • •

The bureau chief at Shiraz was adamant that we not leave for Ahwaz so late in the day. Travel would be slow and we might get caught in the dark. "There are still highway robbers out there that block the

3

road with boulders. They hide in the daytime, but at night they come out," he warned. But the schedule had to be kept; the bureau chief had delayed us long enough with his enthusiastic tours and demonstrations. Seeing that we were not to be reasoned with, he offered us his official Jeep. It was newer than the one we had driven; perhaps he thought a new car would act as a talisman against danger. My father consulted with his assigned driver, Seifpoor, who agreed that a mechanical breakdown would be less likely in a newer car. He would leave our car in Shiraz for maintenance and arrange for a swap later.

My father always took Seifpoor's advice on these matters. They were both drivers of the old school who would not dare drive a car they could not fix themselves with the tools in the trunk. But Seifpoor had gone on to become a professional, while my father had abandoned his romanticism for prestige and power. They understood and envied each other as only true friends could. Seifpoor was a small, quiet man, very respectful in his tones, even when he spoke to street beggars. He was also a mechanic of the highest ability. When I think of him, a trumpet comes to mind. Why? Because his name is similar in pronunciation to the word *sheipoor,* which is the Persian word for "trumpet." He was not loud or brassy; the association is an accident caused by a novice brain groping for meanings of sounds. Nevertheless, there he is, filed amidst tubas, trombones, flutes, and such.

The sun was already low in the sky when we started. Soon the heavy dust in our wake acquired the sad orange glow of an ending day. A temporary wistfulness overcame us as our souls prepared for nightfall. Seifpoor drove and my father talked about his truck-driving days. My mother rolled some cheese and greens in pieces of bread and fed everyone.

Darkness happens quickly in the desert. Seifpoor was telling us how after sunset inexperienced drivers wander from the road and go round and round in circles until they run out of fuel. The next day, lost in the desert, they die of heatstroke. I would be one of them, I thought, because I could not tell the difference between the supposed road and the rest of the landscape. Seifpoor would not get lost, we were all sure; even as the terrain became rockier and hillier, he kept his eyes intently and confidently on the road.

We began a steep climb. The Jeep was whining pitifully for more

4

power. Seifpoor leaned down and engaged the overdrive. He never did that in the city. I had asked him several times about the little sticks next to the big stick shift, and he had said that those were for when the car needed to scale mountains or climb walls of fortresses. We must be climbing mountains in the moonlight, I thought, and began to imagine seeing fortresses growing out of the heights of craggy mountains.

At the steepest point of the climb, as we went around a tightly pinched corner, Seifpoor suddenly put on the brakes. Even though the corner was sharp and the wheels had little purchase on the dirt road, he controlled the skid. The car stopped inches from a boulder on the road. A little less skill and we would have fallen off the road or collided with the rock.

Boulders were lined strategically across our path. There could not have been too many places like this on the road. The robbers had chosen this spot cleverly. On one side of the boulders there was a drop, on the other a hill. The incline was so steep that it consumed all the strength of the engine so that it would not be easy for a car to push the rocks out of the way.

The dust from the skid was hovering quietly across the beams. All was silent. My mother pulled me closer to her. She reached down and pulled the cheese knife from the food basket. She held the little weapon so tightly that I thought the handle would spit the blade out.

Seifpoor broke the silence. "Shall I turn around, sir?"

"Can you?" my father wondered. The road was hardly wider than the car.

"It may take a while," Seifpoor said.

My father thought for a few seconds. Then he said, "Before you start, go out and clean the dust off the sides of the car."

Seifpoor hesitated; this was a bad time to find out that his boss was crazy. But he took a piece of mechanic's cloth from under his seat and went out to clean the car. As he wiped, he realized why he had been ordered to do so, for I saw him pick up speed and then hop over to the other side to clean it. The stencilled emblem on the side of the car proudly proclaimed "THE IMPERIAL GOVERNMENT OF IRAN." And just in case the thieves were illiterate (as was likely), a fierce lion waving a sword paraded amid the letters. There we were, at night, between nowhere, probably surrounded by cutthroats, but we were armed with a powerful symbol, the talisman the bureau chief had given us.

Seifpoor got in the car to begin the turnaround maneuvers. A single man approached from behind. He looked inside the rear window, then came up to the driver's side. I could not see his face. Seifpoor did not let him speak first.

"Someone has made the road impassable. Help us clear it!" Seifpoor bellowed in a tone I did not know he was capable of.

The man had noticed the emblem on the car. My father sat puffed up as far as his chest would allow. He did not appear interested in the conversation of subordinates. The man went over to the boulders. Seifpoor waited to make sure his help was needed and then went out to give a hand. After the road was cleared, the man said that there was an inn a few kilometers from here and asked if we could give him a ride. Seifpoor agreed on the condition that the man ride on the fender. The man obeyed. We rode many kilometers with him breathing dust on our fender, such was the power of our talisman. When the inn came in sight, the man jumped off the car and disappeared.

At the inn we sat at the tables in the garden. There was a refreshing smell of water and mud all around. My father and Seifpoor ordered hot tea. My mother and I shared a Coca-Cola. While we were recovering, we heard a commotion. Three men were teaching a blind man to ride a bicycle. The blind man crashed into walls and bounced into bumps. The three men were laughing cordially and patting him on the back so that the blind man felt obligated to smile even as he was tormented. Seifpoor and my father were indignant but tried to ignore the affair altogether. My mother finally ordered them to go and "say something to them."

After they were launched on their crusade, I asked my mother, "What if the thieves had not gotten scared by our sign? What if the cheese knife had been too small and you could not kill all the thieves? What would you have done then?"

"I would have waited until they threatened you, then I would have turned into a vicious she-lion and attacked them and torn open their flesh."

I felt better about our lucky break. I cuddled closer to my mother,

6

secure in the feeling that if ever motherland failed me, mother would not.

When we reached the city of Ahwaz, we were finally in oil country. Not much farther south, the port city of Abadan bakes in the torrid climate of the Persian Gulf. The flaming stacks of the refinery, like giant candles on a vast birthday cake, invite the nation to make a wish. Upon this wealth lay our future. Or so it seemed at the time. As it turned out, we did not find our national purpose in being the world's fuel tank. Abadan and Ahwaz remained important, but our devotions were attracted by another city much farther to the north. In the seminary at the city of Qom, a religious uprising was nurtured into a national revolution. Many years before those events, I went to Qom to visit my grandfather.

An Incident in Qom

Far, far away, hovering above the horizon, the turquoise minarets of Qom belly dance in a haze of hot dust. In their midst, the golden dome of the Hazrat Masoomeh mosque glows like a setting sun, while a hotter star at its zenith turns the road below into a ribbon of percolating tar. A speeding bus loaded with pilgrims shrieks toward its destination. But Qom does not become nearer even as its gates are reached; the feeling of farawayness persists, and the soul continues to scan the distances as though bewildered by an extrasensory illusion.

The source of this psychic anomaly is the shrine of Hazrat Masoomeh, the virgin sister of the Eighth Imam. She is buried in Qom. From here she found her way to heaven, and it is along this trodden path that multitudes yearn to undertake their own journey into the other world. The earth beneath Qom is dense with corpses, the sky above awash with sounds of mournful praying. Not every soul is helped by the praying; sometimes, in the guise of winds, lost spirits whistle through the alleys, whorling the dust of their own remains into hideous shapes.

My mother is buried in Qom. She was young when she died. My father once took me to visit her grave. I was happy to see that her spirit had not lingered in the dust; like all kindhearted people, she had found her way to heaven quickly.

This story happened four years before my mother died, when her healthy body was busily preparing a new life for survival outside the womb.

• • •

Aunt Tooran's husband, Farabi, had recently bought a Volkswagen beetle. This was our family's first car, and for the first few weeks there was hardly a conversation of importance that did not involve this new acquisition. This car affected me greatly; since its arrival, the familiar world had felt refreshingly different. Something I could not quite put my finger on—it was like the world had a new haircut. This VW isolated in me a feeling that, for the first time, I identified as pride. It also brought about my first conscious judgment of beauty. The creamy gray of its paint, the bulge of the shiny hubcaps, the raspberry purr of its engine, the woolly smell of its upholstery have not been encoded as abstract mnemonics in my brain, but have stayed alive and raw, a territory for sensual time travel.

My cousin Daryoosh, Farabi's son, four years older than I and of closer kinship to the car, was my guide in understanding the more abstract aspects of the vehicle. He explained things like the VW mandala. It aroused profound mysticism in me to learn that the cryptics represented the sounds "vee" and "double u" in the alphabet of the people that created the object. I never questioned Daryoosh's credentials as an authority on Western languages. His explanation of the castle and beast emblem on the horn button varied hourly, but I never exhausted his creativity in all the hundreds of times I asked about the design.

We both still remember the license plate number: 2811. That such a small number could uniquely identify a vehicle makes it even more meaningful to me: in my private numerology, 2811 represents a

9

young and uncrowded world where a still tame technology is only beginning its reverse evolution from domesticated to wild. In this world, the fires in the machines have not yet begun to win their battle against air, water, and earth.

The first long trip with the car was to Qom to visit the graves of my paternal grandparents. We packed as many people as volume and compressibility would allow. There was Farabi, my father, my mother, my unborn brother, Daryoosh, his sister, Aunt Monavar, Aunt Tooran, a servant, and myself. My mother was uncomfortable with the crowding, so various permutations of seating were tested. The one that worked best was to have my mother sit in the front passenger seat. This had some drawbacks: whoever sat in the front had to have me sit on her or his lap; my mother did not wish me to sit on my unborn sibling throughout the trip. Also, the front passenger seat was my father's place for reasons of social rank and his function as crew. An experienced flight engineer was needed to provide counsel to the pilot when important decisions needed to be made. My father recommended gearshifts and passing speeds, warned of bad drivers ahead or behind, and listened for odd sounds from the engine. So my mother was given the least uncomfortable of the rear seats.

My mother's fortunes changed quickly because just as we were leaving the southern limits of Tehran to head for Qom, we spotted on the sidewalk my father's oldest and largest sister, Effat. My mother took the opportunity and insisted that she would sacrifice her seat so that Effat could go instead. This accident, she suggested, must have been arranged by my deceased grandparents because they wanted to see Effat. Conveniently, my mother's sister lived nearby and so the matter was settled. My mother was extracted and Effat and her shopping basket were forced in.

The road to Qom is flat, but the conversation is often lively. It is not until the last half-hour of the trip that the level desert grill picks up a few gentle warps, dry creek beds appear, and the eye is prepared for visual events. At the peak of one of these warps the dome of the Hazrat Masoomeh mosque suddenly becomes visible in the distance, radiating the spell of Qom upon the visitor. Normal conversation dies down and contemplation begins.

Seekers of alms gather at this vantage point so that the pilgrim can stop and display generosity in front of God. This time there was only a beggar child on the road. She stretched out her palm. We did not stop but drove on as my father explained the significance of this point on the road. I tracked the child until she vanished. I wondered how she had gotten there; it was several hours' walk away from anything and she would die if she stayed outside too long. But she stood there like a disappointed hitchhiker unaware of the heat, until her image shimmered and disappeared.

We reached Qom at midday. The women got off to visit the shrine and my grandmother who is buried in a cemetery nearby. Farabi drove me and my father to another cemetery and dropped us off. It was a secluded cemetery with a clay and straw wall around it. The gate was too small for a public place. Inside, the ground was tiled with dusty gravestones. The Prophet warned against gravestones that can become idols: not even a mound of earth must mark a grave. Death is final; whatever happens afterward is God's business. But even the Prophet's own grave has a mosque around it. The strength of his advice has faded with time, heeded only in that the gravestones are placed flat with the ground.

We walked over the gravestones to a place next to the wall. There was a large plaster bulge on the wall as though the wall were pregnant. My father stopped and said solemnly that this was where my grandfather is buried. His ritualistic tone told me that I was being presented to my ancestor.

My father had had very few personal experiences with his father. He told me that fathers had little to do with children in those times. My grandfather had died of appendicitis as a young man. What I know about him comes from one story repeated over and over again: One cold and snowy day my father went to school in shoes so worn-out that the snow melted between his toes. During class he was called to the office and there stood his father with a new pair of shoes for him. It seems that the whole structure of my father's enormous love for his father is built from material from this single event. We never entered a shoe store without his repeating this story. I had accepted the ritual as part of shoe buying and did not protest the repetitions. Today I do not buy shoes without performing the ritual mentally, and I intend to pass it on to my children when they are old enough.

That day, as we stood in front of the bulge, he retold the shoe story. Afterward, I asked him why grandfather was hanging off the side of a wall like that. He told me another story.

When my father was seven years old, Grandfather became ill. There was an American missionary hospital in their town where he was diagnosed as having appendicitis. The head mullah advised against his being treated by Christians. Should he die, he told the family, he would certainly go to hell. Instead, he was brought home where the mullah wrote some verses of the Koran on a piece of paper and dissolved the ink from the writing in a glass of water. My grandfather was given a drink of this medicine, but he died anyway.

In his will he had asked to be buried in Qom; he had even bought himself a burial plot there. But it was wintertime, the family had suddenly become poor, and the trip to Qom would take weeks by camel. He was temporarily buried nearby until more favorable conditions presided. A few months later, a young child in the family had a dream in which an angry grandfather had said, "May your dreams remain forever unfulfilled."

The family acted quickly. Property was sold at bargain prices. Grandfather was disinterred and brought to Qom by caravan. When he arrived, it was discovered that someone else had mistakenly been buried in his plot. By Islamic law, a grave site cannot be reused for forty years. So Grandfather's remains were plastered to the wall of the cemetery until his burial plot would be ready for him.

I asked to see the original grave site. My father was reluctant, but I insisted. I found it strange to see him yield to my urgings. Usually no meant no on pain of the whip. But it seemed that, here, I had power over him. He was being forced to submit to my demand. I saw the reason for his reluctance as soon as I saw the grave site—the date on the gravestone was recent. The forty years had gone by and no one had remembered; someone else was buried at the site and the forty-year timer was reset. I was furious. How dare they bury someone else in my grandfather's grave! Did they not know that he was waiting? I did not believe that even the first burial had been a mistake. With the help of my newfound power, I turned my rancor against my father. Why had he not remembered? Someone was being dishonest. Why was he not taking the matter up with the law? All through the raving, my father was reciting a quiet prayer over the new gravestone. His eyes were closed. He was gently tapping a pebble on the stone. When he got up, the issue was closed. He became a rock and would not discuss the matter anymore. I had lost my new power over him.

We walked back downtown without talking, but I had the impression that he was conversing with someone I could not see. The strength of his grip on my hand was modulated by the rhythm of this conversation. At the city we visited the shrine and Grandmother's grave. Afterward we entered a mosque to listen to a sermon. We took off our shoes and sat among a large crowd of pilgrims gathered in front of a young mullah who had a powerful gift for oratory. He was telling them about our VW. He was saying that Westerners work very hard and dangerously close with matter to earn the power of technology, but in the process they poison their own spirits. The Moslem, he said, should enjoy the leisure of such technology without exposing himself to its spiritual hazards. Here was something Daryoosh had not told me. I could not wait to enlighten him. The people that created our car were in spiritual agony because of it. We Moslems are cleverer than they, for we get the car while they get the punishment.

On the way to joining the others, I asked my father if, on his trips to Europe, he had noticed that the natives suffered spiritually. He seemed irritated that I had understood what the mullah was saying. Could he not enjoy a sermon without having his son exposed to ideas that make dangerous toys? Failing to parry my inquisitiveness, he finally said, "What the mullah said is good for grown-ups and bad for children." That did not answer my question, so I badgered him some more. Then he said briefly and grudgingly, "If they are not allowed into heaven, they can always build their own." He would explain no further, and I could not understand why he was so angry and evasive.

We joined up with the others for a very late lunch of steamed rice and kabobs. The women had bought a few kilos of *sowhan*, a crisp and thin candy that Qom is famous for and that pilgrims are obligated to buy for relatives that stay behind. Farabi and Daryoosh, having been left by themselves, had found a unique batch of *doogh* (a sour yogurt drink concocted to quench the desert thirst) and had bought the whole goatskin from the street vendor. The women were noisily angry at Farabi for not remembering that there would be no room in the car for the goatskin, which was so fat it would not fit in the trunk. We tried drinking as much of it as we could, but even though we became bloated, the goatskin remained as hale and chubby as ever. Finally, Daryoosh suggested we tie the doogh to the hood of the car. Farabi was ordered to go and buy some rope. When he returned, we secured the goatskin and started on our way back to Tehran.

. . .

We had not gone far. Listening to the lullaby of the engine, I was falling sleep on my father's lap. Half awake, I could still hear Tooran berating her husband over the goatskin. Then Daryoosh said something about a speeding bus breathing down our necks. My father's voice, muffled through my drowsy nerves, told Farabi to move over and let the bus go by. Suddenly there was a heavy jolt, and a scraping, gurgling sound. I was waking up slowly. There were screams rumbling in my eardrums, a dizzy merry-go-round feeling, followed by weight-lessness. I opened my eyes; the ground was slowly coming toward the windshield; we were falling nose first into a dry creek bed. My body was shielding my father like an airbag. I tried to twist out of this deadly position, but I felt his grip tighten painfully around my waist as he lifted me up in the tumble and tossed me to the rear of the car. In slow motion he began to cover his face with his arms, but there was no time; a powerful impact crumpled the frame of the vehicle, forcing the windshield to shatter explosively in his face. Instantly, his face became a mass of bubbling blood. Then I lost consciousness.

I remember being propped up limply against a boulder in the creek bed. The burst goatskin had splattered yogurt all around us. There were strangers from the road pulling the injured out of the car. They made a makeshift stretcher out of a blanket and put my father in it. As they carried him by me, he said mournfully, "My son, did he die?" The strangers looked at each other meaningfully but did not answer him. I started to say that I was not dead. But I could not move. I could not even open my eyes.

When I regained consciousness, I was draped like a raincoat over the back of a car seat. This time I lifted my head to see that my three aunts were in the back seat and my father was lying on their laps. My aunts seemed only slightly injured, but they were wailing over my father. It occurred to me that something terrible had happened, but my first act was to try to show my father how strong I was. I gave him a very loud and cheerful "Hello Father." I said it as though I meant to say "Happy New Year." My aunts hushed me vigorously, but my father yelled at them angrily, "Nothing has happened, nothing has happened, tell me what has happened that you weep as though we are all dead." After that my aunts remained quiet and let my father bleed silently on the good samaritan's car on its way to the Qom hospital.

In the years that followed, my father and I had many disagreements. There were disputes and disappointments, battles and betrayals. I do not see him anymore. But he is a man of the pen and I am sure that he has chronicled in unsent letters my bullheadedness, my silliness, my ingratitude. Someday, after his death, I will open these letters and realize my errors. But I am sure that among all the things that he did for me, he will not remember to mention that a long time ago, when I was very young, he offered his life in exchange for mine.

I still regard our accident in Qom with superstition. What benevolent spirit intervened to spare my mother and my unborn brother? And what had the rest of us done to be deprived of this protection? Iranians temper their spirituality with rational doubt, but omens are difficult to ignore when they come from the direction of Qom. Perhaps Hazrat Masoomeh was offended that we did not stop to pay alms to the beggar girl on the road. That would explain why the oracle chose not to punish Aunt Tooran's girl servant who emerged from the wreck unharmed. This servant, not much older than the wanderer we rebuffed, was excessively burdened in caring for injured family members. Maybe we were chastised, not for any single lapse of charity, but for our general thoughtlessness in treating the less fortunate.

The Golden Girl

Sometimes, in her lighter moods, my Aunt Monavar would say to her girl servant, "Zari, it is a good thing that your name means 'made of gold,' because you are so ugly that if you were made of anything less dear, they would have to throw you away."

Zari's eyes would light up at this. She would say bashfully, "Yes, *khanoum* (Mrs.)," and continue her chores with noticeably more bounce. It was rare that attention was paid to her in a currency other than harsh criticism. The insult was comic relief, a truce in the name of humor.

Monavar had chosen a generous ground for ridicule: Zari's head was essentially a nose with thick hair on the top and the back of it. All other facial features—eyes, mouth, ears—like the mounting of a precious jewel, served to encourage and enhance the nose but otherwise stayed timidly out of the way. She kept her shoulders close to her ears and her arms away from her body as though she had been inflated to this shape. Her bowed legs with knee joints pointing outward gave the impression that she ambulated by leaping. An observer of Zari's carriage would be convinced that she was wearing very uncomfortable undergarments. But I calculate beauty with a crude and limited arithmetic on which much of the universe is wasted. My calculus dismisses as deviant mathematically elegant proportions that express themselves in extraordinary strength and endurance. Among the objects so discarded, I can cite the rhinoceros, the bulldozer and Zari.

I jealously stifled astonishment when I saw that girl pull large buckets of water from the garden pool as though she were powered by diesel. Although I was a little bigger, I could hardly drag a small bucket over the edge of that pool. Pulling the handle with my back arched as far as it would go, my arms creaking with the strain, I fought the pool for the bucket. On the way to the flowerbeds, the bucket dangled and splashed ferociously between my legs. Only when I had wrestled it half empty in this manner was the bucket subdued so I could water the trees with any dignity. When I think of Zari, at first my resentment of her strength is reenacted hormonally. Next, I am cascaded by memories.

I last saw Zari when she was sixteen, but in my mind I always see her as a five-year-old girl. That is how old she was when her father abandoned her to my aunt.

She was squatting just outside the guest room entrance where the shoes are taken off. Her father was sitting inside close to the door sucking tea through lumps of sugar. He had been served hot tea in a large drinking glass with no handles. Protected by dirt, callouses, and low social standing, he had no difficulty tolerating the scalding glass. Aunt Monavar, her husband, her son, and various other relatives sat further inside, sipping tea in dainty, gold-rimmed guest glasses. The fact that children were excluded meant that important negotiations were in progress. We had guessed that the topic of discussion was the girl who sat huddled next to her father's shoes, and we quizzed her mercilessly.

Had we strained to listen, as Zari was doing, we may have gathered enough clues to satisfy our curiosity. As it was, our badgering was keeping us all ignorant of the very gossip that we hoped to hear. Zari, irritated or frightened, did not speak with us, so we concluded that she did not like us and resolved that we would not like her either.

My first act of cruelty to Zari immediately followed this resolution: I craned my neck into the guest room and in my most intrusive manner demanded some of the sweets that were put there for the guests. The interruption could have fetched me a scolding, but as I had calculated, the meeting was too important for that. I was bribed with a piece of *gaz* and hastily dismissed. Gaz is a thick white paste so sweet and sticky that it can rot your teeth and pull them out all at the same time; for this reason it is held especially dear by children. I took the gaz and, overcoming my stinginess, shared it with the other children. I encouraged them to show the girl that she was not to be part of our sharing. My comrades, whether on their own heartless initiative or out of gratitude for the gaz, put on an energetic display of exclusive lip smacking. Zari did not accommodate us by acting the beggar. Instead she huddled even closer to her father's shoes and looked even more frightened. Undaunted, we continued to torment her.

A long time later we heard the commotion that signifies the end of a meeting. The adults emerged from the guest room. Zari's father came out first. He was tucking something into his coat pocket. As he headed for his shoes, Zari stood up eagerly. Her father deliberately did not notice her; he put on his shoes and began saying good-bye to the adults. All the time the procession was moving toward the outside gate. Zari was following her father very closely as though she wanted to be the first out the gate. When the gate was reached, Zari's father faced her solemnly and said, "You will be staying here tonight." He placed his hands firmly on the gate latch as though he thought Zari would bolt through the gate and run home. It was an insensitive gesture, for it was clear that, at that moment, the girl's spirit had suddenly collapsed to her feet like a loose garment. Only her mouth would move:

"Where are you going, Agha?" This was the first time I heard her speak. In all the time I knew her, I do not recall a single utterance from her that was not tainted with the hopeless pleading of her first words.

"I will come back for you tomorrow," mumbled her father as he turned to leave. Meanwhile, Monavar had come forward and clutched Zari tightly by the hand. The father opened the massive iron gate and stepped through. As he disappeared, Monavar shut the gate behind him. The clang of metal still ringing in our ears, we all turned to stare at the five-year-old girl who was hanging off Monavar's arm, panting in fear.

I cannot judge him without the facts. He may have saved his child from chronic starvation. The girl's bowed legs did suggest a poor diet. Zari was certainly too ugly to give away in marriage. A face like that would require a heftier dowry than a possessor of calloused hands could afford. The secret contract may have included an allusion to an adequate dowry when Zari was old enough for marriage. I can only guess. He may have had a prettier daughter he could give away for the money he received for Zari. It is also possible that he just assured himself of a few months' cigarette money. I never found out, for I never saw him again. For all I know, neither did Zari.

The girl belonged entirely to Aunt Monavar, who had a weak heart and was advised by her doctors to limit her activities. Zari performed the tasks that Monavar was forbidden to do. She kept the house clean to its theoretical limits, did the grocery shopping, watered the garden, and, except on special occasions when Monavar's exceptional talents were required, did all the cooking. She performed these tasks under the supervision of a mistress who felt strong resentment at having been displaced as the housekeeper. Monavar could no longer be the subject of praise and applause for the clean house, the good food, and the ironed clothes. Her occasional transgressions into domestic drudgery were met with affectionate but serious scoldings from the relatives. For this reason the better Zari performed, the harsher she was treated. If she did anything less than her best, she was punished.

The balance of Zari's time was spent in waiting for miscellaneous commands. "Zari, get me a pillow," "Zari, go buy some kerosene," "Zari, polish the shoes," "Zari, cut open a watermelon." Outside the house, Zari was my aunt's seeing-eye dog, helping her up the stairs, into the taxi, off the curb, across the street. She was trained to think that if Monavar should die it would be because Zari had failed her. She was ever so watchful that no harm come to her mistress. But sometimes she failed.

19

One morning Zari came back from the marketplace short-changed. Monavar went into a rabid rage and gave her a savage beating with a heavy brass ladle. The child's screaming was broken into an anguished staccato as the thumping forced the air out of her lungs. After the beating, Monavar collapsed into the cushions; she would not answer anyone's calls. Zari, convinced that Monavar was dying, threw herself on the ground and begged Allah to spare her mistress. I remember this incident with my taste buds because that night Zari served us food with the brass ladle. Her knuckles were black-and-blue and yellow from the beating. Her hand shivered. The food had a strange flavor and I remember thinking that it tasted like bruises. I was upset with her for having put her pain into the food.

From then on I noticed that she put her pain into everything she did. It was nauseating to eat the food she had cooked, wear the clothes she had washed, or sit on a carpet she had swept. I could not hide my disdain for Zari and once even received a reprimand from my father for my attitude. He asked me to put myself in her place and see how it would feel. He would have had better results if he had asked me to put a great distance between myself and Zari's suffering. I did not wish to imagine being charged with keeping alive a dying flame in a hurricane, when death blew closer, if I forgot to turn off the faucet or came home from the market shortchanged.

Whether a servant girl comes home shortchanged depends entirely on the integrity of the merchant. Zari was not taught how to count. It is stupid to educate a servant. It spoils her and makes her mind wander from her chores. It raises her expectations of life. Soon she is no longer controllable. This is what happened to Zari: despite all our precautions, she learned to read.

We did not know how. We guessed that she picked it up from other people's servants during our numerous family get-togethers. My Aunt Tooran's servant was particularly suspect because Tooran had a daughter in the first grade who was learning the alphabet. The servant learned to read while baby-sitting this daughter. Her mistress, seeing that her child was getting help with her schoolwork, let this go on over the objections of relatives.

Before her literacy was discovered, Zari was asked to bring the daily paper to the living room every evening after dinner. This was her most pleasant chore and she carried it out most willingly. She knew it was time for stories, debates and reminiscences. There was a liveliness to this part of the evening when the family members, like a pride of lions sharing a meal, contentedly gnawed on their share of the newspaper.

Monavar was very fond of the section called "Accidents." It was the thickest section of the paper and the most thoroughly illustrated. It contained a picturesque guide to yesterday's murders, suicides, car accidents, fires, explosions, and executions. This section also reported on people who had returned from the grave and the testimony of lost siblings of celebrities.

Monavar's husband busied himself with the section entitled "Condolences and Congratulations." It featured, in small print, several pages of obituaries along with flowery expressions of commiseration from friends of the bereaved. There was also a space reserved for commemorations, where people who had lost their beloved long ago published their continuing grief. In the same section and in the same format, promotions were announced: "The well-wishers of Mr. Ali Khalili would like to congratulate him on his well-deserved promotion to the post of Assistant Director of the Worker's Insurance Program."

My aunt's husband had a vision problem that his thick glasses did not completely correct. As a result, his eyes had relegated part of their visual function to the tip of his nose so that he read the lines by running his nose against them. His progress could be followed by watching his head, which acted like a typewriter carriage return at the end of a line. He took his nose off only to turn the page. An occasional gasp of surprise sent the rest of the household scurrying in his direction. A gasp meant that someone we knew had either died or been promoted.

The front-page national news ever assured the reader that an ever-growing nation was being managed by an ever more competent government. It seemed unpatriotic to need this assurance every day, so the adult Iranian rarely showed interest in the front-page section. It was the adolescent who took delight in the super heroic antics of the leaders and the comic-book propaganda style. As a newcomer to this age group, I took a faithful interest in the progress of the construction of Iran's first automobile plants. I combed related articles carefully for clues as to how fast the vehicle would accelerate.

Monavar's only son, Iraj, further along in his teens and about to enter the university, was struck by the economic significance of the endeavor. He agreed enthusiastically with the editors that Iran was quickly becoming a space-age culture. As evidence he pointed to the rocketing levels of pollution that the newspaper proudly compared with those of the major superpower cities. The adults, even though impressed, advised caution and contemplation. Monavar was more encouraging. She even went so far as to suggest that should her son ever find employment outside the earth's atmosphere, she would knit him a spacesuit. Iraj was overly susceptible to Monavar's humor and often reacted explosively at being taken lightly.

I was not so observant as to note Zari's opinion on the modernization issue, but I do remember that it was during one of these family read-togethers that Monavar first suspected the girl's ability to read.

Zari usually peered at the accident page over her mistress's shoulder and expressed curiosity about the pictures of mangled vehicles. "What happened, khanoum?" she would ask nauseously. And Monavar would either dismiss her or give a curt response: "The car ran into a wall. The whole family was in it." "Was the servant in the car too?" Zari often wondered. "Yes, she was killed," Monavar extemporized. "It is good that we do not have a car then," Zari opined. "There are cheaper ways to get rid of a bad servant," Monavar joked and Zari giggled, "Yes, khanoum."

One time, Zari absentmindedly chuckled without provocation. We all looked up: it was out of character for her to be so spontaneous. What was this impudent joviality? Had she gone mad? Monavar's ears pricked and her eyes glowed. She grew scales and became a menacing dragon.

"What are you laughing at?" Monavar asked, probing the cornered intruder.

Zari frantically collected the remnants of her smile, "Why, khanoum? I was not laughing," she said matter-of-factly without the slightest hint that she thought she was in trouble, without the smallest acknowledgement of Monavar's threatening tone.

I mentioned before that I did not like Zari. What I found most exasperating about her was that she was such a brazen liar. Even when faced with overwhelming evidence to the contrary, she clung to her ridiculous stories. Where she failed in imagination and consistency in fabricating her lies, she lavishly atoned with stubborn perseverance in defending them. She did not break down in Perry Mason fashion (the dubbed version of the lawyer's exploits were being shown in Iran at the time) but proclaimed innocence even as the electric chair was activated. Monavar, a seasoned Zari hunter, delighted in the sport offered by this habit.

Now she stared into Zari's eyes for a long time. Not finding anything, she transformed back into human form. "Go sit in the kitchen," she said gruffly and returned to the paper. A few minutes later she started reading to us about a man who could make a tin can sound like any musical instrument whatsoever. He was offering to perform at weddings. We were all guffawing at the idea of a tin can wedding when I saw realization wash the laughter from Monavar's face.

No one but Monavar was convinced by such meager evidence that Zari had learned to read. But my aunt was adamant; she inclined to a hunt at this late hour and the hounds had to be awakened. Interrogation was useless, we all knew, so an elaborate stakeout was masterminded by Monavar that night. Her enthusiasm gradually overwhelmed the rest of us.

Monavar was right. A few days later, Iraj discovered Zari in the guest bathroom. Excitedly, he hollered for everyone to gather so that his testimony would be strengthened by witnesses. I was the first to reach the scene and was mortified by what I saw: pinned to the bathroom wall was a terrified Zari; in her guilty clutches she held the promotions page.

The servant was beaten and banned from the evening read-togethers. From then on care was exercised—however unsuccessfully—that she did not gain access to anything printed. But in Monavar's mind the damage had already been done. She may have been right, for about a year later, Zari started coming home very late from her daily trips to the bakery.

Our suspicions were sluggish to be aroused because it is not unusual to be very late from the bakery. Iranians eat their bread fresh out of the oven. For this reason they buy bread just before the meal. During the lunch and dinner rush hours, the bakery is a place where scores of hungering Iranians lay siege to a gigantic oven that is defended by growling flames and harassed bakers in sweat-drenched tanktops.

The bedlam, the roar, the aroma of fresh bread, the kerosene fumes, the pressure of one's nose against the jostling competition, the flight of blistering flat bread frisbeed to its famished owner, the yelling and complaining, the fights and bribes—the bakery is a testing ground, an artillery range where the Iranian's survival weaponry is developed and tested. The crafty and the cunning learn to get their bread quickly and to go home to a hot meal. The weak and the stupid are merely stepped upon.

Iraj was a growing young man and as he grew, so did his bakery skills. He would pass the bribe to the baker, then complain angrily that he had been waiting for hours. This gave the baker the opportunity to give him his bread without being lynched. I was not so skilled. Many times Iraj had to be sent after me to the baker's to find out what was taking me so long. How humiliated I felt as time after time I followed him home and watched in shame as he victoriously tossed to the kitchen the bread I was meant to capture.

In Iran buying bread takes as much effort and perseverance as earning it, but a few rules of conduct do apply: gendarmes, the handicapped, women with infants, and some mullahs are exempted from the games. Their meals do not get cold waiting for bread. Zari belonged to the league of servant girls who, traditionally, came home late and trampled. But of late she had been exceptionally tardy and appeared unusually unkempt on her arrival. Her excuse for being late and dishevelled could not be challenged. The bakery is a battlefront and every day the war intensifies. But she could not explain the other peculiarity: the times when she came home late, her *chador* (a cloth draped over the head and body) was covered with large damp spots. She was questioned on the damp chador several times but never seriously; Monavar was too bitterly familiar with Zari's style of hiding. The girl insisted that her chador was not wet. When she was beaten, she would confess that she had been crying in her chador. When it was pointed out that the chador was too wet for that, she stated flatly again that the chador was not wet. Monavar was not well enough for detective work, but Iraj, bright, agile, and eager to prove himself, would tail her.

Zari was not easy prey even for Iraj. She was mastering the art of deception at a rate proportional to her physical growth. She had hurried through puberty. The romance novels that were confiscated from her at the rate of several a month were getting harder and harder to find. She covered her tracks well when she knew she was being hunted. Iraj came home several weeks from his gumshoeing with nothing to report. He was becoming convinced that Zari was innocent. Monavar reminded him that while Zari had not done anything out of the ordinary on her way to the bakery the last few weeks, she had not come home with a damp chador either. Iraj redoubled his efforts and one day arrived with exciting news. A friend of his, enlisted because he was unknown to Zari, had seen the girl slip into a house not far from the bakery.

Zari was kept in the dark about this discovery until preparations could be made. The next day Iraj went asking around the neighborhood and found out that the tenants of the house were two young men. Not much else was known about them.

After this news, the excitement around the house intensified to its hysterical maximum. An animated Monavar was busy on the telephone conferring with relatives. Children were put under orders not to discuss anything with the servants. It was common knowledge that servants used young children to gather intelligence. Children who could not be trusted were loaded with misinformation. My younger brother was told that a suitor had been found for Zari. He told Zari that she was about to be married off.

The next Friday there was a large gathering of relatives in the guest room. That this was an important meeting was evidenced by the presence of the important men in the family. The highest-ranking member of the patriarchy was Mr. Khalili, the oft-promoted Assistant Director of the Worker's Insurance Program. He was so revered that he did not have to remove his shoes when entering the expensively carpeted guest room. When, out of humility, he did remove his shoes, cries of hospitable protest bade him put them back on. He did not appear interested in or even aware of the reason for his presence. The clan needed its important men and here he was, drinking tea and carrying on important conversation with the other important men.

Zari, possibly thinking that her engagement was about to be announced, was in a happy mood. She chatted cordially with the other servants in the kitchen, and when the time came offered pastries in her most pleasant manner. Monavar chose the moment well. When Zari was offering the tray of tea glasses to Mr. Khalili, Monavar addressed him loudly above the din.

"Mr. Khalili, you are the wisest. Would you ask Zari where she goes when we send her out to the bakery?"

There was instant quiet across the room. Everyone was staring at Zari, looking for her reaction. Monavar's intent was to overwhelm the stubborn servant girl with the importance of the men in front of her. It was a brilliant opening move. If Zari could be cracked, Monavar was the only one who could do it. Mr. Khalili took his time formulating the question while Zari stood shivering with the tray.

Finally Khalili spoke. "Girl," he said, "have you done something to bring shame to your mistress?"

This was no ordinary inquisitor. His voice was hypnotic with importance. No servant girl would be given the opportunity to lie to this man. That is why the question was worded as it was: ambiguously. Zari lowered her head in submission and whimpered, "No sir."

"It is not me you should convince. It is your mistress," he said, nodding in the direction of Monavar. He had done his part as she had intended him to, surged his power through the girl and thrown her, dazed, back at Monavar.

Zari broke down crying. She threw herself at Monavar's feet and vehemently denied hiding anything. She invoked Allah, Mohammad, Ali, Hossein, Hassan, and whatever imams there are to testify as to her truthfulness. All the while Zari was performing her scene, Monavar sat listening with a mocking smile on her face. When Zari was done, Monavar, still patient, said calmly, "Go get the Koran." It was time to bear God's power on the girl. Zari hesitated for a moment and then turned to obey, but Monavar stopped her. "Do you know what happens if someone touches the Koran who just lied in the name of God, the Prophet, and the imams?"

Zari's face dropped. "No, khanoum."

"The Koran will suddenly jump and stick to her hand and burn like the fires of hell and will never come off."

All present agreed in a rumbling murmur. Zari quivered as she stood; she was holding her torso with both arms as though hanging on to a soul which was about to abandon her body in this moment of terror. "Now go get the Koran!" Monavar shouted.

Zari began murmuring louder and louder, "God is merciful, God is merciful, God is merciful." She walked out to get the Koran. We heard her chanting all the way to the hall closet and all the way back. She stepped into the guest room still chanting, still shivering. She held the Koran. With trembling hands, she put the book in Monavar's lap and stopped chanting.

"Do you swear by the Koran that you have told us everything and that you are not lying?" Monavar asked.

"Yes, khanoum," Zari said.

"All right, we will see." She looked to Mr. Khalili who stood up on cue, and with him the entire assembly rose. "Put on your chador. We are going out," Monavar ordered.

"Where are we going, khanoum?"

"To the gendarmerie. If you are lying, they will throw you in jail."

"I am not lying. The Koran knows that."

"If you are not lying, then those two men are. They told me what you let them do to you."

This was the first time Zari heard the accusation. She was stunned for a moment. Then she did something no one was prepared for: her bowels loosened on the expensive carpet—and in the presence of the Koran.

The noisy procession on its way to the gendarmerie was impressive. The women's chadors were flailing in the wind like banners: the storming of the Bastille was being reenacted. This analogy was not lost on the children who occasionally ran to the front of the rabble and excitedly ordered the charge with make-believe swords and trumpets. Ghobad, one of my adult cousins (and the black sheep) was chosen to lead the group. While drunk, Ghobad had been the object of numerous high-speed police car pursuits and in the instances when he had not succeeded in his evasion, he had had the opportunity to become intimately familiar with police matters. Fortunately, the important men in his family had helped minimize these opportunities, giving Ghobad the perhaps not inaccurate impression that there is a way out of everything. He carried himself with the irritating confidence of a gambler who flaunts his cheating skills and challenges the world to catch him. (The incident in which he accidentally killed a man was still in the future, but there was a way out of that too.) Today, he carries himself with the same smugness, now justified by his very large bank balance.

The gendarmerie was an ordinary house rented by the government and used with little modification as a police station. The sentry with the Bronze Age rifle and the red, white, and green flag hoisted on the brick wall identified the house as a gendarmerie. Inside the walls the empty pool and the dry garden beds were the only clues that this was not a residence. Fortunately, our group was the only plaintiff; had there been another group in that small house, we may have had to wait outside and the dramatic flow would have been interrupted.

A small gendarmerie has a complement of four: the sentry, the chief, the deputy, and the tea server. The latter also doubles as housekeeper. It was the old tea server who showed us into the office. He was dressed in servant fashion: several layers of unrelated clothing, sleeves rolled up to the shoulders, shrunken but baggy pants with an elastic waist, cloth shoes. He had the odor of a kerosene stove about him and in this respect was like Zari and all other servants. The tea server seemed interested in what we had to say and stayed through the final act.

The chief was a middle-aged heavyweight with a thick mustache. His uniform had been made when he was much thinner. Noting that some of the men in our party were wearing good suits, he ordered tea to be brought for the men. The women waited in the hall. The first few minutes before tea was served were spent in amenities and introductions. It is impolite and imprudent to talk business before credentials are presented.

"This is Mr. Khalili, Assistant Director of the Worker's Insurance Program," Ghobad explains lavishly to the chief.

"Yes, yes, my niece's husband's brother works there. He has spoken well of you several times. I wonder if you know his name—Mahmood Ravani," the chief says eagerly.

"Of course," says Mr. Khalili, " a bright young man. I did not know he was related to you. Did he not have a son born to him recently?"

"A daughter," says the chief apologetically, "but the next one will surely be a son."

The men all murmur "*Enshallah*" (God willing). Tea is served amidst more small talk; finally Ghobad begins his approach.

"Colonel" (it is customary to address a uniformed man by several ranks above what his stripes suggest), "it is so fortunate that your servant is a man. Girl servants are very troublesome, as everyone here can testify."

"Please tell me of this trouble, maybe I can help," the chief says.

Ghobad leans conspiratorially over the chief's desk and speaks in very secretive tones. "The chastity of one of our servant girls has been severely compromised by two bachelors in the neighborhood."

The colonel shakes his head thoughtfully at the tragedy. "How bad is this compromise? Is the girl. . . . " He trails off with a knowing gesture; he does not want to say "pregnant."

"Fortunately not, but the girl is suffering greatly; she has no one but us. She looks up to us for these things and we look up to you," Ghobad explains, using tones and gestures that imply he is asking a personal favor from the colonel. He is telling him that we have come to him, not because we think it is his duty to help us, but because we believe him to be a man of honesty, compassion, and wisdom. We would go to him for guidance even if he were not an officer of the law, but we are so fortunate that he happens to be one. The colonel accepts all of this gracefully and resolves not to disappoint us. He appears genuinely upset for us and wishes to know the details.

"What has the girl told you?" he asks.

"Nothing. The poor illiterate girl is not feeling well. We are not sure if she even understands what has happened to her, the criminals being so much older than she is. We saw her go into their house several times. She came out an hour later, looking very untidy and upset. Her chador was wrinkled and damp when she came home and there are bruises on her body. The women in the hall have seen the bruises and can tell you."

"I do not doubt their truthfulness. We will go at once to settle this matter as soon as my deputy has taken down the complaint."

Ghobad and the deputy go to another desk and huddle over a long sheet of paper while the colonel and the important men sip more tea and discuss the perils that face a lonely servant girl. The colonel has been personally involved in several cases, all of them horror stories. Mr. Khalili explains that the girl's mistress had trained her exceptionally well in housekeeping and that he was intending to contribute a chrome samovar to the girl's dowry. Alas, her reputation has been tarnished such that hundreds of gold samovars cannot remedy.

After much tea, the conversation has wandered to the topic of the rising price of real estate, but the complaint is finally documented. The procession, this time led by Iraj and the colonel, flanked by Khalili et al., heads toward the house where the two men live. The deputy and the sentry carry the rear. On the colonel's orders, the tea server has locked up the gendarmerie. He is following far behind so as not to be noticed by his superiors.

By far the favorite spectator sport in Iran is the "street event": two beggars beating each other over the rights to a choice spot on the sidewalk, a woman who has caught a pickpocket in the act and is screaming for a witness, a man yelling angrily at another because the latter has brushed the former's wife not quite by accident, a street vendor under assault for not taking back bad merchandise. Surrounded by many tons of compressed humanity, I have stood on my toes, craned my neck and elbowed my way into hundreds of such street events. Attending street disputes is my pastime; it is in this way that I feel the least different from the norms of my culture.

The procession we had created was an extraordinary street event, and even the least curious, the most deviant from the norm, were not able to resist attending. By the time we reached the target house, our numbers had grown manyfold. Passersby, expecting action at the end of the march, curiously walked along with us, gathering gossip. The neighborhood children were weaving in and out of the crowd like aerial acrobats staging a dogfight. Several bicyclists, a motorcyclist, street vendors, beggars, shoppers, and shop owners had all dropped their businesses and volunteered in the colonel's army. The storyteller should not exaggerate an event that is already out of proportion in the original; nevertheless, it is my sincere speculation that, given our national tendency to riot when assembled in large groups, had the house been just one block further, the numbers would have snow-balled past critical mass and staged a violent demonstration.

The colonel signalled the halt; we had reached our destination. The door of the residence fit in the space between a fabric store and a stationery store. The residence itself sat on top of the two stores; perhaps it was originally intended to be storage space for the businesses below. It was not a house as I had imagined it. The colonel knocked loudly and ceremoniously. The person who opened the door must have seen or heard us coming. He looked pale and scared and terribly puzzled even as he opened the door. I expected to see two scarred murderer types snarling with curled lips and brandishing daggers. The man at the door was a handsome, bespectacled young man with a clean haircut. He was dressed in his house pyjamas and had a pencil behind his ear. His roommate soon joined him and they both stood shoulder to shoulder, in total bewilderment at what was staged before them.

"Name and place of occupation," the colonel demanded.

They gave their names. They were students at the University of Tehran. They had come from Shiraz.

"Have you any relatives in Tehran?"

They had none. This was important for the colonel. It would have complicated matters if these two produced their own arsenal of important men. Thus reassured, the colonel pushed on with an angry speech: "Have you no shame that you recklessly take advantage of a servant girl who is too stupid to know better? And you call yourselves students, seekers of knowledge. . . . "

Meanwhile Zari was ceremoniously being brought to the front by Monavar and her attendants in grief. Soon, there would be no obstacle between the criminals and the accusing finger. The crowd was parting solemnly to make way for them. Zari's face was buried in Monavar's side. She was sobbing while Monavar gently consoled her on their funereal progress to the door. When Monavar looked up at the two men, her teary eyes burned angrily and accusingly, but they softened into an expression of motherly grief as she bent her head to caress away Zari's tears. Exactly when this transformation in their relationship occurred, I am at a loss to say. Somewhere in the stream of events, they must have understood that they were now performing in a production written and directed by Ghobad. At the sight of the servant girl, the two men turned cyanotic. It was as though a noose had been tightened with a sudden yank. Frantically, the one with the glasses interrupted the colonel's speech and began explaining.

"Colonel, you are our senior. It is not our place to contradict you. What you know must be the truth, but I swear to my father's soul that we have done nothing untoward to this girl. What has she told you? She is a liar. We are decent people from Moslem families. At least tell us what she has told you."

"She has told us everything," the colonel shouted, "and denying is useless."

"We deny nothing. I swear to the orphans of Karbala, may they bless your children, she did not even so much as take off her chador when she was in our house. . . . "

"So you shamelessly admit that you had her in your house!" the colonel interrupted victoriously.

"Of course. We could not hide anything from you even if we tried. You see, one night we had many guests and friends over for dinner. The next day we saw this girl in the bakery and asked if she would like to sweep the rug and clean up a little for a fair wage. Since then she has been coming in once in a while to dust and do the dishes. That is all. May God strike me mute if I am lying when I say that we never even saw one strand of her hair. We insisted she keep her chador draped around her when we were at home. We are Moslems, we are Shiites."

The mystery of the damp chador had thus been given a plausible explanation. I could imagine Zari clumsily washing and cleaning, all the while a tent wrapped around her head and body to preserve her chastity. It is surprising that she came home as clean and dry as she did and that she had not even once tripped headfirst into the washtub. I cannot be certain of what the colonel was thinking, but I can

32

reconstruct a possible line of thought using as my guide the colonel's subsequent actions and my own experience as an Iranian.

The colonel also saw a simplifying elegance in the way the facts fit this new story. The first thing a man wants from a woman is not sex but a clean house. Besides, these two men, regardless of their proclaimed devotion to Islam, had the opportunity to associate with university women whose virtues are easier and whose appeal harder to resist than that of a servant girl who looks like a miniature rhinoceros and smells like a kerosene stove. Also, quite apart from the horror stories of the servant girl genre in which he had played the role of the hero, the colonel had seen many hysterical accusations that had damaged more lives than the alleged crimes which originated them. After arbitrating so many disputes, a keen sense for truth must develop. I believe that the colonel accepted the two men's version over Ghobad's improvisations.

Had it not been for the eager crowd expecting fast-paced and action-packed justice, the colonel's mind would have been at peace with his conclusion. Had Mr. Khalili not been the Assistant Director of the Worker's Insurance Program, the colonel might have questioned the girl and satisfied the crowd by making a liar out of her. But it did not seem appropriate to make a fool out of such an important man as Mr. Khalili. What would happen if the colonel's niece's brother-in-law, in need of a favor, approached a disappointed Mr. Khalili? Last of all, what law had been broken? What could be proved? This was not something the Khalili clan intended to take to court. The cause was a servant girl and it is understood without words that the price in terms of time and effort and risk to family honor was not worth the cause. They had approached the colonel for justice and it was up to him to come up with the law that had been violated and to administer the punishment.

In reverse order, that is exactly what the colonel did. He took a quick, threatening step toward the first man with the glasses and with all his power and speed delivered an echoing slap across the man's face. The glasses tumbled violently into the air, jerkily reflecting the afternoon sun so that it looked like the colonel had knocked sparks out of him. The crowd roared at the spectacle. After this, further

33

violence would have been anticlimactic. The young man said nothing and stood tight-jawed in punishment like a schoolboy. "One does not engage other people's girlservants without permission!" the colonel declared loudly to the attentive crowd.

The law had spoken. Members of the crowd were already repeating the prohibition. *One does not engage other people's girlservants without permission.* Mr. Khalili was nodding in thoughtful approval. Since the charge itself vindicated them of a more dreaded accusation, the two men themselves zealously embraced the principle, denouncing their own rashness and apologizing obsequiously to the colonel, Mr. Khalili, and the crowd. I have never seen a proposal ratified into law with so little controversy and with such dispatch. The populace, their thirst for action quenched and now equipped with a new guiding principle, was beginning to disperse in cathartic contentment. Our original group started to head back to our house. The two men went inside and closed the door. I cannot even guess what they had to say to each other.

On the way back, the colonel and Mr. Khalili were explaining to each other that they were not so naive as to believe that Zari had not been violated, but in the interest of the girl's future it seemed prudent to create the appearance that nothing scandalous had happened. Monavar was later advised of this and she was pleased to be entrusted with such a life-and-death secret. The incident would be brought up many times and retold in myriad versions: sometimes to demonstrate Zari's ingratitude—had she not been rescued from certain ignominy by a valiant Monavar? sometimes to demonstrate her weak morality—what sort of woman would fornicate with two strange men at once? sometimes to demonstrate how ugly she was—had the two young, single men alone with her in a house not pleaded with her to keep her face covered?

Zari stayed with Monavar until Monavar died. After that, Zari just vanished. Once I asked Iraj of her whereabouts. He said he did not know. I do not believe him. I think he knows a hundred stories that he is not telling me. One of them may even be true.

Of Monavar's small family, Iraj is the only one that I have seen since I left Iran. On his latest business trip to the U.S. he paid me a short visit. He reported that his father was still alive and healthy. Madani was an old man even when Iraj and I were young.

I was happy to see Iraj; in Iran older cousins take on brotherly responsibilities for their younger cousins, and since Iraj was an only child, he was particularly eager to fashion a younger brother out of me. Certainly many of the stories of my youth involve learning to deal with cousin Iraj.

He is now a very successful businessman and educator. But he has not changed much. Still bright, arrogant, delightful to tease, and prone to illusions, he is exactly as I remember him from our childhood.

During his visit, we did not discuss the past much. I was more curious about the ongoing war between Iran and Iraq, and he was willing to impress me with his analysis. He intellectualized on the subject at length, giving me opinions already wrung dry by newspaper editorials. Other than that, he preferred to make small talk. He had gone to see the doctor about chest pains; the doctor said it was nothing, he should take a vacation. Finally I got him to talk about how he and his family were handling the war. He told me about the helpless feeling he had during rocket attacks on Tehran. When the sky grumbled in the wake of a falling rocket, all he could do was tell his children to stay away from the windows. Then he changed the subject again and prattled on about the positive aspects of war: it unites the population, strengthens national character, stimulates the economy, gives youth responsibility, etc. When the martial music was over, I told him that if *my* children lived under falling rockets, I too would develop chest pains. His reaction was unexpected. He drooped into a thoughtful posture, his eyes moistened, and his body braced itself for something awful. I thought, for once, he would tell me what was on his mind. But, nimbly, like a matador, he danced out of Truth's way to restore the natural balance of denial. He went on to rave about the wonderful management information system he was implementing for his clients.

The Dog

For a few years during my early childhood, we lived in a large house in the desert suburbs of Tehran. It was a desolate area consisting of a planned shopping center, several planned streets, our house, and a real estate office. A source of great puzzlement to me was watching my father and the real estate man run their fingers across the map on the wall and talk about "the boulevard," "the bathhouse," "the fountain square."

"Where is the fountain square?" I would ask on the way back from tea at the real estate office.

"You are walking on it," my father would say. I looked down and saw dust, pebbles, and thorny desert weed that even the roaming goat herds left alone. My father was right though. One day I was able to see the fountain square, and as I grew older, I saw more and more of what had been invisible before.

36

Even though the settlement was growing, my mother felt uncomfortable living in such a desolate area. The gendarmerie close by was no consolation; the desert was too large to patrol. My father tipped the gendarmes now and then to keep them interested in our safety, but he was away too much and the tips did not suffice.

The nights when my father was away until late, my mother and I kept away the chill of fear by roasting pumpkin seeds in the kitchen. But after a while even pumpkin seeds could not provide the protection we needed. I was not sure what it was we were scared of.

"Robbers," my mother had said. Robbers were humanoids whose faces were shiny bubbles of tar; they slithered underground like earthworms and crept over walls like lizards. The only weapon effective against them was the heavy pick handle my father kept under his pillow. My great-uncle Khandaii, a retired officer of the famous Cossack Brigade, had offered his side arm. But firearms were illegal and we would rather be robbed than deal with the secret police.

The solution came knocking on our door one starlit evening. Two teenage boys stood outside the gate holding a gunnysack that wriggled and growled.

"What is it?" my mother asked.

"Khanoum, your husband is away a lot and this area is not safe. You need a good guard dog." My mother stepped back slightly. Dogs are *najes* (unclean) to Moslems. Undaunted, the boys said they would like to come in and close the gate so the dog could be shown. My mother was reluctant but curious, and she knew I would pester her.

"Let the poor beast out so it can breathe a minute," my mother said. The boys had been clever to put the dog in the sack. They upended the sack over the garden sod. With a yelp and a growl the puppy fell out. A few seconds to recover from the tumble and he was on his feet assessing his surroundings. He did not wish to run away; it was too dark and scary, but he kept growling just the same in case he had misjudged our characters.

"Where did you get him?" my mother asked.

"In the *jube* (irrigation duct). The water master was about to run water through and he would have drowned." The puppy had stopped growling. He had just finished nibbling on himself and had settled comfortably with his chin on the ground, eyeing the conversation.

"Only eight rials," one of the boys said.

My mother had not mentioned anything about buying the dog, but she countered with, "Two rials, I am short on shopping money."

"But Mom, you said you had saved . . . ," I started to say.

"Besides, it is too small to be any good as a guard dog," my mom said, loud enough to drown me out.

"But Mom. . . . "

"Go sit inside," she ordered. I did not obey, but stayed inconspicuous from then on.

"It will grow to be a very big dog. You can tell by the size of the ears," one boy said. After all, elephants have big ears.

"Three rials. If you want you can want, if you don't want you don't have to want (take it or leave it)."

"Five rials and we won't have to put it back in the jube."

The dog was scratching himself behind the ear and grunting in syncopated rhythm.

"Go get my money," my mother told me, but I was already halfway back with her coin purse. She took out three rials and extended them to the boys. They stepped back, offended.

"We said five rials," they sniffed.

"I said three rials," my mother reminded.

The boys conferred. Finally one of them said, "We have twenty rials to go to the movies, but we need two bus tickets to get there. We need at least four rials." My mother sighed and pulled out a ten-rial piece.

"Do you have change?" She was testing them. The boys searched themselves, but all they had was the twenty-rial bill. They looked up crestfallen.

"Keep the change. Buy yourselves some pumpkin seeds at the movies," she said. The boys leaped in joy and vanished. I would see them again in a year.

When my father came home, I was already asleep. Usually my mother let me stay up to keep her company, but that night she put me to bed early so I would not botch her little trick on my father. She let him go through the nightly security inspection of the house without telling him about the dog. I woke up to my father's yelp. He ran back to the house stumbling and panting, "There is someone in the coal bin. Get the pick handle!"

The dog lived in the coal bin at the far end of the yard. There he was protected from the elements and was not close enough to the house to make our residence unclean. He grew to be very big. I wonder if he did not look big because I was so little, but witness the following dialogue between Aunt Tooran and her husband Farabi:

Tooran: "Jafar's dog is monstrous. I have not seen any dog get so big."

Farabi: "When I was a boy in the village, Hashem Khan kept a guard dog that was perhaps bigger. It may have been as big as a small mule."

Tooran: "Then it was not bigger, because Jafar's dog is as big as a large mule."

It would be an insult to humanity and to Islam to honor a dog with a name. The dog was referred to as "Dog" in conversation. But it was hard to get the animal's attention with this word, so whenever the dog's presence became necessary, he was summoned by a mnemonic I often used: "Hapoo," kidspeak for "one who barks."

Each morning, Hapoo emerged from the coal bin and agitated his fur into giving up a giant cloud of coal dust. When the air cleared, there remained a yawning stretch of black and white dog. By the time we finished breakfast, the yawn would be completed and Hapoo would walk up to the gate and wait to be let out. He would return at about ten o'clock and stay home until midafternoon, when my father came back for lunch. The agreement was that the dog would always be home after sundown.

Hapoo was an excellent watchdog. He kept away the robbers, the mailman, the garbage man, the water man, the meter reader, the newspaper man, the census taker, and all the vendors. He was also very successful in keeping away friends and relatives. Whenever friends came to see us, they would call from Agha Ali's store down the street to remind us to chain the dog. It was not enough to assure them that the dog did not bite, because he did bite. He bit me regularly even though he tried not to break the skin. What the friends feared more than dog bite, though, was dog hair. Repeated ablutions are necessary to cleanse the effects of contact with a dog. Clothes may have to be thrown away. Give a parched Iranian the choice between a glass of water sniffed by a dog and a glass of radioactive waste, and he will have to think about it.

My father used to amaze his audience with how Americans live with their dogs. He told us dogs are routinely given names in America and that in their grocery stores there is always a section that has dog food and dog toys in it. They were much aghast with surprise. How could anyone make money selling dog food? What a waste of human labor to make food for dogs. Aunt Tooran asked if dogs were permitted in stores and bathhouses. My father explained about special dogs like police dogs and seeing-eye dogs having special privileges. This drew great admiration from the relatives. He said bathhouses were not common in America, but that dogs were given baths with special dog soaps. This drew guffaws from the audience. He also mentioned a dog named Lassie who was so well trained she acted in movies. This had to be a movie trick; surely there was a human inside a dog costume. But my father explained about King Kong and how obvious it was that the beast was not real. He could tell the difference between real beasts and costumes; Lassie was a real dog.

"Did you meet any dogs with doctorates?" Aunt Monavar quipped. One of the relatives present had just received a doctorate, and Aunt Monavar was having difficulty accepting the new order.

My father said, "No, I saw something stranger. I saw a woman kiss a dog on the mouth."

Aunt Monavar spat her tea back in the glass and excused herself to go vomit.

Our dog was sterilized weekly with a can of DDT. This was the wonder powder with the miraculous cleansing effect. I was told that the powder was extremely deadly and never to go near the can. My mother often wondered out loud if DDT did not hurt the dog. "No, dogs are much stronger than humans," my father said. What kept the dog alive was his mighty shake. Immediately after the dusting, he sent waves of powerful vibrations down his body, scattering all the DDT dust for his masters to breathe. I know he shook off most of the poison because his parasites never left him.

The weekly dustings helped keep the relatives from banishing us altogether, but during the four years Hapoo lived with us, their visits to our house were limited. The dog showed his resentment of their attitude by breaking his chain and attacking them. This was mostly for show. He never broke his chain unless one of his masters was around to beat him back. The relatives were not satisfied, however, and always entered our house backs and palms to the wall, muttering prayers.

Hapoo's legend spread across the settlement. He struck fear in the hearts of neighbors, but as long as they remained honest, worked hard for a living, and did not break the law, he did not bite them. He had a civilizing influence in the neighborhood: street fights were quickly abandoned when he appeared, and robberies happened less often. He not only guarded our house but became a policing force in the area. With his black and white markings and great bulk, he could easily be mistaken for a police motorcycle, although no motorcycle engine, however unmuffled, could duplicate Hapoo's gut-shaking barks. Also, the neighbors appreciated him because since his appearance, stray dogs had become scarce.

One day the two teenage businessmen came to our door to give us our money back and reclaim the dog. A dog with such a reputation was worth much more than ten rials. Maybe they had heard the Lassie story and were eyeing the movie business. My mom told them that the dog was attached to us and we would not give him up. The teenage boys said that she was being unfair. My mother countered that we had spent at least ten tomans (one hundred rials) on meat scraps in the last year. The dog was worth at least eleven tomans by her estimate. That should have gotten rid of them; eleven tomans was a very large sum for a teenager. Nevertheless, the boys returned with eleven tomans the next day.

Her ploy having failed, my mother finally took the money and said with great resignation, "All right, he is tied up in the backyard. Go get him."

The boys looked at each other, puzzled. They did not expect to win so easily. They marched off to the back. My mother kept the gate open and waited. Suddenly, we heard Hapoo's explosive roar. But the boys did not run out the front gate as my mother had expected. Concerned, we rushed to the backyard.

There was only the dog, his hackles receding. The boys had vanished. My mother said they scrambled over the wall. I say the dog ate them up, clothes and all. When my father came home for lunch, my mother showed him the eleven tomans. He said he was sure they would be back for their money. But they never came back, adding credence to my belief that Hapoo had eaten the very boys that had saved him from drowning. This was the very antithesis of the Lassie theme—which is why Hapoo never made a movie.

Hapoo was never really friendly nor really hostile to anyone: he was too important to take sides. The one exception was quite dramatic. The dog wagged his tail, whimpered affectionately, and rattled his chains longingly whenever Aunt Tooran's husband, Farabi, came to visit. At the time, Farabi was a dapper young man. He wore expensively tailored suits over Italian shirts and ties. The crease in his trousers ended in shoes shined to an obsidian luster. The only traces of his uncosmopolitan background were his slight Turkish accent and the array of expensive fountain pens displayed across his chest. To match the shoes, he waxed his thick shag of black hair with generous helpings of hair cream.

Farabi did not come to our house often, but after each visit, Hapoo would howl wistfully for hours, until his canine olfaction ceased reminding him of Farabi. Farabi was quite flattered that such a VIP would lose all dignity over him. He attributed it to his rural background. People of the land have a way with animals that city people have forgotten. Aunt Tooran would not let him enjoy his superiority. She was always mocking him for being liked by a dog. Farabi retorted that in all his life only two creatures had hankered after him: the dog and Tooran.

If dogs can pray, Hapoo's prayers were answered. One day, during a gathering at Tooran's house, my mother discovered that she had lost the keys to our gate. A volunteer was needed to climb our walls and get the other key from inside the house. But no one was foolish enough to scale walls guarded by Hapoo. My father was away on a trip in Turkey, and I was too small. I insisted that with help, I could climb over. But if for some reason I was not able to find the key, I would be unable to get out. My mother was out of the question, and everyone else feared being eaten.

42

Tooran demanded that Farabi go over as the dog seemed to like him. Farabi said he did not wish to get his clothes dirty. He also tried various other ploys, but each time he was reminded of all the village stories in which he had tamed the wild bull and brought back the runaway horse. A man has to pay for his bragging someday—Farabi was offering to pay for a locksmith instead. My mother said that locksmiths are useless when there is a growling beast on the other side. She had a knack for persuasion. Everyone was enjoying Farabi's dilemma. I was beginning to wonder if my mother had really lost her key. Did Tooran arrange all this to get back at Farabi for his rural hero snobbery? Finally, his honor at stake and his rural bravado in question, Farabi agreed to go.

Many of us followed him the few steps to our house to watch. Farabi climbed to the top of the wall. Hapoo could be heard whimpering excitedly on the other side; his tail was thumping against the brick wall.

"He must have smelled us coming," Farabi said from the top of the wall. Had he really hoped he could sneak in and out under Hapoo's nose?

"Stop delaying and go get the key!" Tooran said. Hapoo could not agree more: his whimperings now and then broke into howls.

"Tooran, are you sure this is wise?" Farabi was earnestly seeking Tooran's opinion.

"Just get the key! Why are you just sitting there?"

"I am giving the dog time to adjust. I don't want to frighten him."

"Are you going to go or do we have to push you over?"

Farabi went over.

There was a joyous howl of fulfillment. Farabi screamed, "Back, back, animal, back!"

But Hapoo would not hear it. He was a most enthusiastic host.

"Back! Back, you beast! Get lost! Tooran, help! He is licking me! I am not joking!"

"Just go get the key!" Tooran shouted.

"I can't. He is on top of me. Help me, cruel woman!"

There was a great deal of panting and yowling and screaming and name calling. Suddenly it all stopped. Tooran looked concerned for the first time. I was sent over the wall to see. The dog was in front of

43

the coal bin licking his muzzle. Farabi sat sprawled in the garden. He looked quite unharmed, but there was something strange on his head, like a large vegetable brush. Hapoo had licked off all the hair cream but had no use for the rest of him. Farabi was left planted in the garden like a giant thistle.

This "dog lick" form of hairstyle has only recently been appreciated in the United States and Europe. I will mention for the edification of modern hairstylists that they were anticipated by at least thirty years by a little-known Iranian dog. Could Lassie have done better?

It was not until after Hapoo's death that Farabi resumed his village stories. I was beginning to miss them. The newspaper said the city was putting out poison meats to get rid of stray dogs. My father thinks Hapoo was accidentally poisoned by this program. I think the DDT finally got to him. It could have been something else. Anyway, his time was over. The desert where he almost drowned at birth had disappeared. The vast territory he once ruled was now many times busier than the map on the wall of the real estate office.

Some friends still called from Agha Ali's to see if the dog was tied up. "The dog passed away a long time ago," we said.

There would be a solemn pause, then the receiver would say sadly, "May God show him kindness."

Not everyone grieved Hapoo's death. Street vendors, garbage collectors, and others whose jobs had been made hazardous during Hapoo's four-year rule were relieved. One merchant who was genuinely saddened by the news was our butcher. He had been making a little money on the side selling us meat scraps for the dog and so regarded him as a customer. Running shopping errands for my mother, I saw the butcher and other shopkeepers often. Usually, I returned with just the merchandise and some change, but one day I came home with a lesson.

The Butcher

The call to noon prayer was beating down from the sun. A laborer mutters his devotion in the scant shade of a sapling.

> *Guide us along the straight path*
> *The path of those You have favored*
> *Not of those with whom You are angry*
> *Not of those who are lost.*

Enough playing and sightseeing at the marketplace. Time to go home for lunch. I had spent the day watching the grape flies at the fruitseller's shade. They float silently in the fragrant air, their wings blurred around them like halos. They read your mind. Try to grab one and it has already drifted serenely out of the way. No hurry, no panic. They know the future.

On the short walk home memories of the fruitseller's paradise are already being bleached by the sun.

Guide us along the straight path . . .

Why do we need guiding along the straight path? I wonder.

I reach the house, but the gate is locked. I don't feel like knocking; there is an easier way. The neighbors are building their house and there are piles of bricks everywhere. After many trips back and forth I have enough bricks to make a step stool with which to climb the wall into the house. My arms are scraped pink by the effort. I sneak to the kitchen and try to startle my mother.

"You better go put those bricks back before the neighbor sees them," she says.

The next day I pass by the fruitseller's and go straight to the cobbler's tiny shop. A pair of my mother's shoes need mending. The cobbler flashes a "two" with his fingers and goes back to the shoe at hand. His hair and beard look just like the bristles he uses on the shoes.

"I will wait for them here," I say as I pull up a stool. He does not hear me. The walls are covered with unfinished shoes waiting to be soled. They look like faces with their mouths wide open.

"They are shouting at each other," I say, pointing to the walls. The cobbler cannot hear them; he is deaf-mute. He emphatically flashes two fingers again. Come back in two hours. So I walk next door to the butcher's shop to look at the ghastly picture on his window and try to figure out what it means. I hesitate to ask him. Some things are better left alone.

The butcher is a decent man. He has to be, for he is entrusted with doing all our killing. Even though we pass on the act, we are still responsible for the deaths we cause. The killing must be done mercifully and according to the rules of God. The killer must be pure of heart and without malice for the world.

Our butcher was a man of great physical and moral strength. My mother said he reminded her of the legendary champion, Rustam. Rustam was so strong that he asked God to take away some of his strength so that he would not make potholes wherever he walked.

The butcher was very big. Every time he brought down the cleaver, I feared he might split the butcher's block. His burly hands carried the power of life and death. The carcasses hanging on the hooks and the smell of raw meat testified to this. Above the scales was a larger-than-life picture of the first Shiite imam, Ali, who supervised this Judgment-Day atmosphere with a stern but benevolent presence. Across Ali's lap lay his undefeated sword, Zulfaghar.

But the true object of my terror was the picture in the shop window.

A man was chopping off his own arm with a cleaver.

The artwork was eerie, as the man's face had no expression—he stared blankly at the viewer while the blood ran out. This was the butcher's logo. Underneath it the most common name for a butcher shop was beautifully calligraphed: *Javanmard* (man of integrity).

I had asked my mother what the mutilation signified. She had said it was a traditional symbol attesting the butcher's honesty, but she could not explain further.

"Is the butcher honest?" I had asked.

"Yes, he is very honest. We never have to worry about spoiled meat or bad prices."

"He would rather chop off his arm than be dishonest? Is that what his sign means?"

"Yes."

"What about other shopkeepers? What have they vowed to do in case they are dishonest?"

"I don't know."

"What about the cobbler? Did he do something dishonest? Is that what happened to him?"

"I don't know."

"Is that why people kill themselves? Because they have been very dishonest?"

"Look, it is just a picture. It's not worth having nightmares over. Next time you are there, you can ask him what it means."

I did not ask him about it until I was forced to by my conscience.

One day my mother sent me out to buy half a kilo of ground meat. She told me to tell the butcher that she wanted it without any fat. She knew it would be more expensive and gave me extra money to cover it. I got to the butcher shop at the busiest time of the day. One good thing about the butcher was that he, unlike other shopkeepers, helped the customers on a first-come, first-served basis. Status had no meaning for him and he could not be bribed. People knew this about him and respected it. When he asked whose turn it was, instead of the usual elbowing and jostling, he got a unanimous answer from the crowd. People do not lie to an honest man.

This gave great meaning to the picture of Ali above the scales. Ali, the Prophet's son-in-law and one-man army, is known for his uncompromising idealism. His guileless methods were interpreted as lack of political wisdom, and he was passed over three times for succession to Mohammad. When he did finally become caliph, he became an easy target for the assassin as he, like the Prophet, refused bodyguards for himself. Shiites regard him as the true successor to Mohammad and disregard the three caliphs that came before him.

When my turn came up, I asked for half a kilo of ground meat with no fat. The butcher sliced off some meat from a carcass and ground it. Then he wrapped it in wax paper and wrapped that in someone's homework. Sometimes he used newspapers, but because of the Iranian habit of forcing students to copy volumes of text for homework, old notebook paper was as common as newsprint. He gave me the meat and I gave him the money and started to walk out, but he called me back and gave me some change. This was free money; my mother had not expected change. I took the money and immediately spent it on sweets.

When I went home, I did not tell her that she had given me too much money. I worried that she would know I had spent the change on candy and that she would yell at me for it.

Around noontime my mother called me into the kitchen. She asked me if I had told the butcher to put no fat in the meat. I said I had told him.

"I thought he was an honest man. He gave you meat with fat and charged you the higher price," she said sadly.

Now I knew where the extra money came from. In the heat of business he had forgotten about the "no fat" and had given me regular ground meat. But he had *not* charged me the higher price.

48

"We will go there now and straighten this out with him," she said sternly.

I thought about confessing, but I deluded myself into thinking the change had nothing to do with it. After all, *he* made the mistake. How much change had he given me anyway? Or maybe my mother was wrong about the quality of the meat. I was just a victim of the butcher's and my mother's stupidity.

It was still noontime as we set off to straighten out the butcher. The call to prayer was being sung. Across the neighborhood devout supplicants beseeched their maker.

Guide us along the straight path
The path of those You have favored
Not of those with whom You are angry
Not of those who are lost.

I was certainly lost. I was fighting the delusion like a drug, now dispelling it, now overwhelmed by it. When things were clear, I could see that I had done nothing wrong except fail to get permission to buy candy. The butcher made a mistake, I did not know about it, and I bought unauthorized candy. All I had to do was tell my mother and no crime would have been committed. The real crime was still a few minutes in the future, when I would endanger the reputation and livelihood of an honest man. I still had time to avert that.

Guide us along the straight path . . .

When delusion reigned, I felt I had committed a grave, irreversible sin that, paradoxically, others should be blamed for. The straight path was so simple, so forgiving; the other was harsh and muddled. How much more guidance did I need? The prayer did not say "chain us to the straight path." When we reached the shop, the butcher was cleaning the surfaces in preparation for lunch. He usually gathered with the cobbler and the fruitseller in front of the cobbler's shop. They spread their lunch cloth and ate a meal of bread and meat soup. In accordance with tradition, passersby were invited to join them, and in accordance with tradition, the invitation was declined with much apology and gratitude.

My mother told him that when she finished frying the meat, there was too much fat left over and she thought the wrong kind of meat had been sold. She asked if he remembered selling me the meat. The butcher was unclear. He remembered having to call me back to give me some change, but he was too busy at the time to remember more. My mother said that no change would have been involved as she had given me the exact change. This confused the butcher and he decided that he did not remember the incident at all. His changing of his recollection added to my mother's suspicions. Meanwhile, Ali was glowering at me from the top of the scales, his Zulfaghar ready to strike. My face was hot and my fingers felt numb.

Finally, the butcher, who was not one to argue in the absence of evidence, ground the right amount of the right kind of meat, wrapped it in wax paper, wrapped that in someone's homework, and gave it to my mother. She offered to pay for it, but the butcher refused to accept the money and apologized for making the mistake. When we left, he was taking apart the meat grinder in order to clean it again.

On the way back I felt sleepy. My mother asked if I was all right.

"I'm fine," I said weakly.

"Your father will be home in a few more days," she reassured.

"Mother, do you think the butcher was dishonest?" I asked.

"No, I think he really made a mistake."

"How do you know that?"

"Because he gave us the new meat so willingly. If he was a greedy man, he would not have done that. He probably feels very bad."

A terrible thought occurred to me. "Bad enough to chop off his own arm?" I asked urgently.

"I don't think so," she said.

But I was not convinced. She did not know what awful things could happen off the straight path. "I have to go back," I said as I started to run.

"Where are you going, you crazy boy?"

"I have to ask him about the picture," I yelled.

"Ask him later, now is not the time. . . . " She gave up. I was already a whorl of dust.

I was panting and swallowing when I saw the butcher. He was having lunch with the cobbler and the fruitseller. What did I want now?

"Please, help yourself," said the butcher, inviting me to the spread. I just stood for a while.

"Why do you have a picture of the man chopping off his arm?" I finally asked. The cobbler was tapping the fruitseller on the back, asking what was going on. The fruitseller indicated a chopping motion over his own arm and pointed toward the butcher shop. The cobbler smiled and repeated the fruitseller's motions.

"That is the Javanmard," the butcher said. "He cheated Ali."

"Why?" I asked.

"Even when he was caliph, Ali did not believe in servants. One day a man came to the butcher's shop and bought some meat. The butcher put his thumb on the scale and so gave him less meat. Later he found out that the customer was Ali himself. The butcher was so distraught and ashamed that he got rid of the guilty thumb along with the arm," he said.

I was greatly relieved. One did not mutilate oneself for committing a wrong against just anybody. It had to be someone of Ali's stature. Our butcher was safe even if he was to blame himself for the mistake. But I had to be absolutely sure.

"So if one were to cheat someone not as holy as Ali, one would not have to feel so bad?" I asked. Looking back, I see that he interpreted this as a criticism of the moral of the parable. He was transfixed in thought for a long time. The cobbler was tapping the fruitseller again, but the fruitseller could not find the correct gestures; he kept shrugging irritably.

The butcher finally came to life again. "Ali was good at reminding us of the difference between good and bad," he explained.

I was glad I was not so gifted.

"Would he have killed the butcher with Zulfaghar?" I asked.

"No, in fact I think once he found out what the butcher had done, he went to him and healed the arm completely," he said, displaying his arms. I looked carefully at his arms, but there was not even a trace of an injury. "A miracle," he explained.

The fruitseller was able to translate this and the cobbler agreed vigorously. He had something to add to the story, but we could not understand him.

During lunch I told my mother the butcher's story.

51

"Now why couldn't this wait until tomorrow?" she asked, collecting the dishes.

"Mother?"

"Yes?"

"If I were to get some change and not bring it back, what would you do?"

"Did you get change and not bring it back?" She smelled a guilty conscience.

"No, I was just wondering."

"It depends on what I had sent you to buy," she said deviously.

"Like meat for instance."

She pondered this while she did the dishes. When she was done, she donned her chador and asked me to put on my shoes.

"Where are we going?" I wondered.

"To the butcher's," she said curtly. "You are going to apologize and give him the money we owe him."

"It was *his* mistake," I protested guiltily.

"And you stood there all that time, under Ali's eyes, and watched him grind us the new meat without saying anything."

I followed her dolorously out the gate. I could tell she was upset because she was walking fast and did not care if her chador blew around. But halfway there she changed her mind and with a swish of her chador ordered me to follow her back home.

"Why are we going back, Mother?"

"If this gets out, they will never trust you at the marketplace again," she said angrily.

"So we are not going to apologize?"

"Of course you will apologize. You are going to give him your summer homework so he can wrap his meat in it."

The summer homework filled two whole notebooks. The school had made us copy the entire second grade text. Completing it had been a torturous task and a major accomplishment. My mother had patiently encouraged me to get it out of the way early in the vacation so that it would not loom over me all summer.

"What will I tell the teacher?" I begged.

"You will either do the homework again or face whatever you get for not having it. Or maybe instead of the homework you can show her the composition you are going to write."

"We did not have to write any compositions," I whined.

"You are going to write one explaining why you don't have your homework."

So, for the fourth time that day I went to the butcher shop. It was still quiet at the marketplace; the butcher was taking a nap. He woke up to my shuffling and chuckled groggily when he saw me.

"I was looking for you in the skies but I find you on earth (long time no see)," he said.

I gave him my notebooks and told him that my mother said he could wrap meat in them. He thanked my mother and apologized again for the mistake. My mother had told me not to discuss that with him, so I left quickly.

Within a few days, scraps of my homework, wrapped around chunks of lamb, found their way into kitchens across the neighborhood.

I opted for writing the composition explaining the publication of my homework. My mother signed it. The teacher accepted it enthusiastically, and while other students were writing "How I spent my summer vacation," I was permitted to memorize the opening verses of the Koran. I had heard it many times before and knew the meaning, but I did not have it memorized. It goes:

Guide us along the straight path
The path of those You have favored . . .

A few summers later, the butcher became involved in the religious uprising against the Shah. He tacked a small picture of Khomeini next to Ali and Zulfaghar and would not take it down. His customers, including my mother, urged him not to be so foolish.

"Was Ali foolish to refuse bodyguards?" he asked.

"You are not Ali, you are just a butcher. Khomeini is gone, exiled. At least hide his picture behind Ali's picture."

When he disappeared, we all worried that he would never come back. But a few days later, he opened his shop again and, as far as I know, never hid anything anywhere.

Khomeini lost his first battle with the Shah, but he came back fifteen years later to destroy the corrupt monarchy. He was perceived by most Iranians to be a man of unrelenting integrity, much like how I remember the butcher. It was easy to believe that under Khomeini's leadership Iran would be cleansed of its corruptions. The greedy and the dishonest would no longer have the advantage over hardworking citizens grateful to God for their daily bread. Khomeini's refusal to compromise with what he thought to be evil eliminated the riddles of our conscience. The line between Good and Evil became as sharp as the slice of a sword. And so the blade promised to establish the laws of Heaven on the land.

How many incarnations of Hell have been conjured by those that would live in Heaven?

The Alcoholic

"Let me show you how to play backgammon. If you are ever broke, you can make yourself some money." My Uncle Nosrat and I sat on a carpeted platform next to a stream of rushing snowmelt. A watermelon, wedged between boulders, waited in the icy water. The backgammon board lay between us, shattered by sunlight and leaf shadow. The shifting breeze blew now from the charcoal grill, now from the teapot over the samovar. When it blew from Uncle Nosrat's direction, it brought the smell of alcohol.

"What if I lose?" I asked. "It is all luck, isn't it?"

"It is all luck if you don't know how to play," said *Amoo* (uncle) Nosrat, taking a sip from his glass of vodka. "Do you know who invented backgammon?"

"People," I said. It had not occurred to me that games were invented by specific persons.

"The wise Bozorgmehr invented it. He was the grand vizier of Anoshirvan the Just. One day a messenger from India came to the Iranian court bearing no message other than a board game he called *chaturanga*. Does that name sound familiar?"

"It sounds like *shatranj* (chess)," I guessed.

"Right. Bozorgmehr spent many days riddling the message, and finally he figured it out. The message was: 'Life is the battle of reason against reason.' In response he sent back backgammon, so as to say, 'Yes, but willy-nilly, chance is always the third player.'"

Amoo Nosrat knew that my father had forbidden me to play games of chance, but during the family picnics, when my father was absent, he sat me down with a deck of cards or a backgammon board and taught me how to gamble.

"Your father is naive," said Amoo Nosrat of his younger brother. "Games of chance hone a child's intelligence much better than games of pure strategy."

"He is just worried that I may become addicted to gambling. He thinks it may be hereditary."

"I didn't think he gambled," said Amoo Nosrat in surprise.

"He means *you*," I clarified.

Amoo Nosrat laughed. "It may be contagious, but it is not hereditary. Your father should be worried that you do not gamble *enough*. Of course, he has done well playing it safe and not risking anything, but I think he has just been lucky so far. Fate will get you whether you gamble or not."

My uncle had strange gambling habits. Sometimes he used his unusually shrewd mind to arrive at the correct odds and then deliberately avoided the most sensible play. He found life most precious at the moments when expectations failed.

"These are little miracles," he explained. "No different from the big miracles except for size."

I asked him why, if he liked to challenge fate, he did not play games of pure chance. He said he was not so favored as to win an all-out war against the odds.

"Sometimes you hold the dice and you know you'd better go along with common sense. But sometimes you feel like you are given permission to do what you want. Have you ever felt that way?"

"No," I confessed. "I believe we should always do what is most reasonable."

"In that case you should take back your last play," he said, disappointedly rearranging the pucks. "It is not the most reasonable move." He flicked up another cigarette and lit it, mumbling through the smoke something derogatory about my father's views on heredity.

When Amoo Nosrat was drunk, he felt free to challenge his fortunes more often. Sometimes when I went to visit him at the gas station he managed, I found him leaning against the wall next to the "no smoking" sign, puffing thoughtfully on a cigarette. I tried to get him to quit smoking—mainly to prevent an explosion—but the relatives were more worried about his drinking. They were sure that if he kept it up, sooner or later he would be hit by a car.

The blame for his drinking was given to his wife Shahla.

"Can you blame him? With a wife like that?" I often overheard. I do not know what Shahla had done to drive her husband to alcoholism; all I know is that Nosrat's sisters resented Shahla for laying claim to their older brother. The younger brother had been claimed by my mother, who was not so hated as Shahla. Perhaps this was because my mother always lost her territorial battles, while Shahla scored major victories. Years ago she had convinced Nosrat that now that his sisters were all married, he no longer needed to worry over them. It was time he concentrated his efforts on his own wife and children.

With the burden of the relatives off his shoulders and with Shahla's encouragement, Nosrat had been able to start a small grocery store and apply his powerful acumen in the world of business. His facility with figures was already well known; he could multiply and divide in his head. But he surprised even himself with his intuitive sense of consumer psychology.

"If it is not the best cheese you have ever had, bring it back. But it is a morning cheese—best with hot, crisp bread." "Same batch of tea as served in the parliament building." "Pomegranate sauce purifies the blood. Keeps you less tired."

Soon, his customers were too many for his little store. He worked from dawn till past midnight to keep ahead of the accounting, the inventory, and the orderings. He enjoyed the salesmanship and the socializing; customers came to him from other neighborhoods to chat while they bought their bulk rice and tea. But the ever-increasing paperwork cluttered Nosrat's happiness. Hired help brought its own problems: payroll, training, discipline, and theft. As the business grew, Nosrat found that he did less and less of what he enjoyed and more and more of what he dreaded.

His attempts to slow down the business—shorten the hours and reduce the inventory—met with scoldings from his wife and the relatives. He should be expanding, they advised. What sane person throws away a thriving business? The store had taken on a life of its own; quickly it became more of a burden than the relatives had ever been. Nosrat was stuck: fortune shone on him doggedly wherever he went, never setting long enough for him to close his eyes and rest. Meanwhile, everyone judged him harshly for being so ungrateful for God's kindness.

Shahla's brother Ezzat was the exception. He was a Sufi, trained in the philosophy of devotion and contentment. He alone listened with understanding to Nosrat's complaints about the monster of financial success. Ezzat was a locomotive engineer with tall tales of bridges, mountains, rivers, and starry nights. His life was my uncle's envy. Nosrat wished dearly to rid himself of his hyperactive luck so that he too could abandon the eyestrain of red and black ink to focus his mind on infinity.

The relatives, while appreciative of Nosrat's Sufi tendencies, were confused by the extent of his sincerity. That sort of philosophy is for the unfortunate, a remedy for the trampled souls of the down-trodden, not a libation with which to celebrate worldly achievements. The wealthy should dabble in such thinking so as not to become the spiritual inferior of the poor, but it is foolish to empty the gold out of one's pockets just so the garment is a better fit.

Of all his critics, Nosrat himself was the harshest. He realized that as head of a large family, his life was not entirely his own. Out of fairness he usually did what seemed most reasonable—make more money. As an escape, he fantasized with Ezzat about getting a job with the railroad or even becoming a bus driver. But any time he fantasized, his wife would go into fits of reason.

"What if you become ill? Are you not going to be sorry that you do not have more money stashed away so that at least your daughters will have a good dowry? You are throwing away your children's bread. Why feel bad about money? You are not stealing it, you are an honest businessman. How much money do you think you are making, anyway, that you feel you can do with less? What if we have more children?"

Ezzat interceded for him. "He is not serious. He is just dreaming. Do you begrudge him even his dreams?"

"Dear Ezzat, what sort of a sane man dreams of becoming a bus driver that my husband should be the second?" Shahla argued.

I was too young at the time to understand Nosrat's dilemma. Why did he not work as a bus driver and ask to get paid as much as a merchant? I am still not clear why the rules of the game are written as they are. Why did Nosrat, who always rolled such a perfect game, want to change the rules? And why, having failed, did he begin to destroy himself with alcohol?

During his drinking years Nosrat went to the mosque regularly. He would drink himself to shame, then go to the mosque and repent until he shamed himself to drink. His early morning customers, tired of waiting outside the closed store for their breakfast cheese, went to other merchants. His late-night patrons, no longer assured of the lively midnight chats, abandoned him to his vodka. The little store that once stocked everything from green zippers to dried lima beans now contained a few half-empty bags of rice which only the cockroaches seemed to fancy. What savings there were he safely gambled away so that nothing could rise from the ashes of the business.

One night, early in Nosrat's drinking career, we heard a frantic knocking on our gate.

"Who is it?" my mother asked suspiciously.

"Asylum, asylum," came Shahla's terror-stricken voice. My mother opened the gate immediately. In stumbled Shahla, wearing no chador over her house clothes. Obviously, she had left her house in some urgency.

"What happened to you?" worried my mother, closing the gate.

"It is Nosrat. He has been drinking. He is after me with a belt." Shahla started to relate the story when there came another loud knocking on the gate.

"Shhh, it is Nosrat," Shahla whispered urgently. "For the love of God tell him I am not here."

My mother waited a few seconds, then asked loudly, "Who is it?"

"I know you are in there, Shahla," yelled Nosrat. "Come on out or I will break down the gate!"

"Oh, it's you, Nosrat Khan. Shahla is not here."

"Then open the gate."

"I can't, you are too drunk."

"Then I will climb the walls."

"You are too drunk to climb walls. You will fall on your head. Go home. If Shahla comes here, I will tell her you are looking for her."

Nosrat tried to climb the walls, but as my mother had predicted, he fell on his head. Finally my mother had an idea.

"Nosrat Khan, Shahla may have gone to Tooran's house. Why don't you check there?" If anyone could handle Nosrat, it was his sister Tooran. She would think of some way to keep him out of trouble until he sobered up. Nosrat went away. My mother listened at the gate to make sure, then invited Shahla in for some ice water. There Shahla told us how Nosrat had invited a dog for dinner.

Nosrat had put his belt around the stray dog's neck and had dragged him, whimpering and nipping, into the house.

"Sir dog, guest of the house," he announced. "Prepare the guest room." Shahla quickly sent the children out the back door to the neighbor's house. Then she went back, crying, to the matter at hand.

"Nosrat, get that filthy dog out of my house, or I will throw water on you!" she said angrily. The dog was willing to leave, but Nosrat would not let go.

"This is the luckiest dog in the world. No more sleeping in the streets, no more rummaging in the trash. From now on he sleeps in the softest beds and eats the tenderest meats."

"Nosrat, for God's sake, you have bites all over your arms. Let the poor beast go. It is very frightened."

"Ungrateful animal. He does not know how good he has it. Tea for my ungrateful guest. And hurry, woman."

"It will be weeks before the house is clean again," Shahla wept. "Please get it out of the house."

"No, this dog will wear my best coats and put on my best shoes." He took off his shoes and while trying to put them on the dog, lost his grip on the belt. The dog started running from room to room looking for an exit. "Stupid beast, appreciate what I am offering you. Other dogs would die to be in your place. Shahla, into the kitchen. Sir dog would like eggplant stew as only you know how to make."

"I am leaving the house right now. You can clean up when you are sober."

"Into the kitchen, I said. Eggplants for sir dog."

"Then take him to a restaurant. I am not cooking for a dog."

"Eggplants or I will beat you."

"Beat me if you want, but I am leaving right now."

Nosrat raised the belt.

"Not with that belt!" Shahla shouted, bolting away. "It's touched a dog!"

"How dare you insult the honored guest!" Nosrat bellowed as he chased after her. Shahla dodged his drunken lashings and ran out the door toward our house, Nosrat stumbling after her.

We sheltered Shahla until she calculated it was time to go and find Nosrat. His dog bites needed bandaging, and everything in the house had to be washed. As we walked Shahla to our gate, my mother asked her how the business was doing. Shahla said it was not doing well and that she wished it would hurry up and go under.

After the store closed, Nosrat found the management job at the gas station. He continued to drink, though not as much, and he kept up his visits to the mosque. We all worried for him when he went out, as he never looked where he was going when he was drunk. Miracle after miracle helped him survive his meanderings across busy streets. But one night his luck gave him a respite. He was hit by a car and badly hurt. His body was cast in plaster, and he lay like a fallen statue for six months until he recovered. When he was released from the hospital, he had stopped drinking altogether. After that, he spent a quiet life visiting the mosque and chatting with Ezzat about the peaceful ways of the Sufi.

After Uncle Nosrat died, Shahla went on to become rich again. The relatives continued their backbiting with innuendos that she acquired her wealth through usury. Collecting interest is forbidden by the Koran and looked down upon in practice. When Shahla died, her children spent their inheritance in accordance with their father's inclinations. Their mother's genes remained helplessly recessive as contentment whittled away the excess.

My mother's older brother, Mahmood, was more like my father in temperament. This is why my father's side of the family rarely socialized with my mother's side; the rivalry between Mahmood and my father kept the two clans cool toward each other. The stress of isolation wore on my mother's nerves, tinting with apprehension memories of my rare visits to my mother's relatives.

The Old Woman Upstairs

On the first day of spring my mother brought out the new clothes she had bought for my older brother. I did not have an older brother, but my mother did not know that; she always bought her son clothes that did not fit him.

"I wish your father was not away so much so he could see you in your *Nowrooz* (New Year's) clothes. We will send him a picture," she said.

"Mom, these clothes are too big, especially the shoes—they go 'hulff, hulff' when I walk. Look at my sleeves, I can't see my thumbs."

"You'll grow into them," she said absently as she tucked in a hemline on my pants and stood back critically. "I'll have to hem them. Take them off."

"What about my shoes?" I asked, climbing out of my pants.

"I'll give you some thicker socks."

"That's OK, I'll just wear my old shoes inside the new ones."

My mother looked up, pins between her lips. "If the rest of you grew as fast as your mouth, you'd be wearing your dad's clothes."

"Whose house are we going to?" I asked, scratching both knees.

On the first day of Nowrooz, the relatives, well groomed and dressed in new clothes, gather to celebrate at the house of a high-ranking clan member. It is a crowded affair. Every time the doorbell announces an imminent addition to the multitude, there is much excited guessing as to who it may be. Then the door is opened like a gift. In walks another family, smiling as they are loudly welcomed by those already present. The busy conversation is warmed by continuously replenished heaps of fruits, nuts and pastries. Traffic of scalding tea is heavy and dangerous.

Nowrooz is a time of newness, good feelings, and altruism. The servants are given new rags to wear, and old grudges are dissolved to make room for new ones. Iranians commemorate the rebirth of the world by bringing together symbols of regeneration arranged on a decorative cloth thrown over the carpet. These symbols often include eggs, sprouting grass, newly minted coins, apples, garlic, vinegar, a variety of spices, mirrors, and goldfish in a bowl. Traditionally, seven of these items have names that begin with the s sound and are known as *haftsin*. The word *haftsin* is composed of *haft*, meaning seven, and *sin*, meaning s, literally "seven s." The Iranian word for "green" (*sabz*) is powerfully sibilant and perhaps this is why the "s" sound has come to symbolize spring, freshness, and rebirth. Our ancestors viewed the cycle of life and death as part of the perpetual moral battle between universal good and universal evil. The haftsin custom dates back to the pre-Islamic Zoroastrian philosophy, and Moslem Iranians observe it with a slight mental apology to Allah. But just so we do not regress too far into pre-Islamic (and purportedly pagan) customs, the haftsin spread also prominently displays a symbol from a later time in our history: the Koran, which performs the miracle of preventing the seven "sins" from being trampled in the colliding cross-traffic of guests.

"We are going to Bayani's house. Do you remember them?" replied my mother.

"The seven sisters in a house?" I asked.

"Six now. Soroor married your uncle Mahmood, remember?"

"No, I was not born when they got married."

"Don't call them the seven sisters when we are there. Bayani is very sore about having no sons."

"All right."

"Was it really that long ago that Mahmood and Soroor were married?" she sighed, staring out the window.

"How should *I* know?"

"I wasn't asking you," she said smiling.

Since my father was abroad, we were spending the day with my mother's clan, who usually celebrated Nowrooz in the very large house belonging to my uncle's in-laws.

"Don't forget. When people give you money, say thank you and don't grab. And don't keep counting your Nowrooz money in front of people." All the way on the bus my mother instructed me in the ways of grace and gratitude. "Ask me if you want something, don't just take it because your cousins did. Keep your shirt clean. Don't call anybody a monkey," she continued as we got off the bus and onto the sidewalk.

"Another thing," she said as we entered a damp alley, "the grandmother has had a stroke. She is very old. You have not seen anyone so old. Don't get scared and don't stare. She shakes and cannot speak anymore."

"Why does she shake and not speak?"

"She has been shaking for a long time, but recently she had a stroke and lost her speech."

"Why doesn't she wish to speak anymore?"

"She *wants* to speak, she just can't."

"Why can't she?"

"She's old and very sick. You are too young to be told about these things," my mother said impatiently.

"Why is she old?"

"I don't know. People grow old after a while."

"Will you grow old?"

"Yes, everyone grows old."

"Will I grow old?"

"God granting. I ask that of Him all the time."

"Why do you wish me to be old?" I asked in alarm.

"It means I pray that, God forbid, you do not die young."

"Why don't you pray I do not die at all?"

"It is not good to pray against nature. We can only pray for kindness."

"Will I be able to speak when I am old?"

"Of course, and stop driving me crazy with your questions."

"What if I have a stroke?" I did not really know what "stroke" meant.

"God forbid. Now no more babbling," she said as we turned into an alley.

The long alley was kept dark by unfriendly walls that kicked us in the ear with the clicking of our own shoes. Clumps of dirty ice, leftovers from yesterday's winter, still survived in the frigid space between the walls. We walked inside this winter sandwich until we came to a gate.

My mother clanged the doorbell. A servant opened the door. People could be heard laughing inside, but the oppressive hugeness of the house flattened the laughter into moans. It was not a welcoming house: the tiles, the walls, the stucco asked for credentials. The steps were mean giants that threatened to trip children. Even the felicitations of Nowrooz, the hugs, the cousins, the jokings, and the sweets could not warm the house. I kept feeling that something was the matter.

"Where is the old woman that shakes?" I asked loudly of my mother.

"Shhhhhh," she whispered. "I haven't seen her yet. I told you not to discuss her."

"You said not to stare, " I protested and then whispered, "Did she die?"

"I would have known," said my mother. "Unless. . . . "

"Unless what?"

"Nothing."

"Tell me."

"Unless she died today. Oh, how awkward for them if she died on Nowrooz."

"Why don't you ask them?"

"It is improper. If they want us to know, they will tell us. And don't try to keep your ears open," she warned.

Lunch was served. Mounds of herbed rice and platters of Caspian fish were brought out of the cavernous basement kitchen. The aroma of herbs exploded in the house. Seemeen and Safieh, the youngest of the seven sisters, both in their early teens, helped the servants bring out the dishes. The rest of the unmarried sisters, Soheila, Soosan, Soodabeh and Saroya, stayed in the kitchen to put finishing touches on their masterpieces. My mother's youngest brother was a bachelor. It was important to impress upon him the need to follow his older brother's lead and marry one of the sisters (he waited until Safieh became old enough and married *her*).

During lunch one of the guests finally brought up the question. "How is Khanoum-Jan doing? Is she recovering well?"

Soheila, one of the older sisters, answered. "Grandmother's stroke has left her without speech. We have moved her upstairs so that our noise does not bother her."

"Will she be brought down for lunch?" my mother asked.

"Grandmother does not wish to see anyone. She has made it clear," Soheila said.

"How does she communicate?" someone asked.

"Well, she is mostly paralyzed and cannot speak, but fortunately, Seemeen and Safieh understand her." The two were sitting next to me at the lunch spread. They smiled bashfully at Soheila's compliment.

"Does she know it is Nowrooz?" someone asked.

"She doesn't know if it is day or night," Seemeen replied. There was a short silence.

"What does Khanoum-Jan eat?" I asked Seemeen.

"Children, " she said, widening her eyes. I told my mother I wished to go home. This drew laughter. Soheila chided her younger sister for being mean, but, though I was irked with Seemeen, it was not her joke that had upset me. I needed an excuse to ask to leave that house. I continued to bug my mother about leaving.

"Your uncle is giving us a ride home. We will not leave until after dinner," my mother said.

"But it will be dark here by then."

"It will be dark everywhere."

After a late dinner, the children went outside to play. I stayed inside, hoping to pressure my mother into leaving sooner. With the children expelled and the adults surfeited, the house was more at peace. The din of the party had subsided into a digestive quiet. I tried to shake the slight hissing in my ears that I attributed to the sudden quieting. But it would not go away. My ears were not ringing. There was a very high-pitched hissing sound that permeated the house.

"Do you hear that?" I asked my mother.

She cocked her head in various directions and said, "Hear what?"

"Sssssss," I said.

She listened a little more and said, "No, you are probably sleepy. We will go home soon." She put my head on her lap and stroked it. I wriggled out and went looking for the source of the hissing. I could not tell where it came from, but it was louder at the staircase. Khanoum-Jan, I thought.

Slowly I scaled the stairs. The hissing was getting louder. It was shriller than any sound I had heard before, but there was so little of it that it was not painful. Upstairs a row of tall and hostile doors stood guard in the hall. One of them was ajar. In the darkness inside sat an old woman glowing white and blue. She was propped up in bed. Her body was limp except for her right leg which, like a restless child, could not be still. Her eyes, fixed and full of all the things her tongue could not say anymore, were begging the curtains to part. Soheila, bathed in the same shifting glow, sat next to her, caressingly braiding the old woman's hair. Occasionally, a mumbling voice said something from inside the room.

Lured by the hiss and now drawn by the light, I moved closer and, for the first time in my life, I saw a television.

I craned my neck to get a better look. Seemeen and Safieh, possessed by the glow, lay arched in front of the set like a pair of charmed cobras. Soheila noticed me standing at the door. She brightened. "Have you seen a television before? It is new," she said.

I was still under the spell of the new thing that pretended like it belonged on the haftsin spread by hissing the promise of rejuvenation and hope, "sssssss." It was new and alive, but not like eggs and sprouting grass—it made the air musty. Outside, on the other side of the thick curtains, spring was only a day old. The air had the crispness of youth, and eternity twinkled assuringly in the starlit sky. The hopeful cycle of life and death was feverish this time of year. The dying woman's gaze, blocked by the thuggish curtains and pulled by the falsely hissing eye that had cast a spell on her offspring, fought desperately to break through. The awful feeling I had been having about the house was coming from this room.

"Come watch it with us," said Soheila.

I walked in and sat on the carpet near the door, my eyes half on the shaking woman and half on the hissing box. Don't stare, I remembered being told.

"Did you have a good dinner?" Soheila asked.

"Yes, thank you," I said cautiously.

"Soheila, be quiet. I'm watching," complained Safieh. But Soheila ignored her.

"Your mom says your father will be home soon. Have you asked him to bring you anything?" she asked.

"Soheila, if you wish to talk, go outside. Grandmother needs it quiet in here," Seemeen griped without taking her eyes off the box.

Khanoum-Jan's eyes slowly drifted away from the curtain toward me. With great effort she raised one arm in my direction and moved her lips.

"What is it, Grandma?" Soheila asked. Seemeen and Safieh swung back irritably.

Khanoum-Jan's body tightened. She started to say something but managed only a few grotesque vowels. Part way through her sentence she collapsed and emptied her lungs with a great sigh. But she kept her eyes on me. A short laughter emanated from the glowing box.

"She is disturbed. She wishes him to leave, " Seemeen said curtly. That was not the correct interpretation. I had a strong feeling Khanoum-Jan was trying to ask me a question. Soheila had said Seemeen and Safieh understood their grandmother, but this was clearly not the case. Did Khanoum-Jan really not wish to have visitors? She *knew* it was Nowrooz. Perhaps she had wanted to be brought down so she could celebrate Nowrooz with us and see all the children.

"Is that right, Grandma? Do you want him to go?" Soheila asked. Khanoum-Jan said nothing. Her eyes rolled back toward the curtain. Soheila looked at me pleadingly. I understood and left the room, puzzled as to what Khanoum-Jan was trying to ask me and why Seemeen and Safieh wished me to leave.

* * *

"Grandma wants to know whose child he is," said Safieh, confirming my own guess.

"Oh," said Soheila. "He is Mansooreh's son. Remember her, Grandma? Mahmood's sister. She has been married eight years now. Would you like to see her again? Seemeen, go tell Mansooreh Grandma wants her to say hello." Seemen skipped out of the room to obey.

In this version Khanoum-Jan's eyes are not trying to rip the curtain open.

Sometimes I remember it this way.

The Iran I remember was caught in the awkward transition between the old and the new. There is nothing unfamiliar in that; the symbols on the haftsin spread attest to an ancient acknowledgement that change is the way of things. But the sensible poetry of natural transformation—the sprouting seed, the egg—were no longer the appropriate metaphors for the discontinuities that our family was experiencing. The fractured way in which our thoughts and traditions adapted to each new whim of Progress can be more appropriately compared to the jarring reality shift of a commercial break.

The Children's Show

"He is just tiny dots of light; there is nothing back there but vacuum," explained cousin Iraj. He knew how television worked and tried to demystify it for me. I did not understand what he said, but his motivation was clear to me: he wished to replace my amazement at television with awe for his understanding of it. I would give him no such satisfaction and kept myself frustratingly stupid. The presence of television made this state easy to achieve and impossible to recover from.

"If what you say about the antenna is true, then disconnecting it should obliterate the picture," I reasoned. Iraj did the disconnection and the picture became very fuzzy.

"You see," he said with great showmanship, "the picture is obliterated."

"Not completely though, it seems the purpose of the antenna is to clean the picture like windshield wipers on a car," I concluded.

Iraj saw red; his voice became squeaky as he swallowed the urge to choke me. "You will never be on the children's show. You are too stupid," he screamed. He meant the part of the TV show where they lined up bright children and asked them difficult questions:

"Are bats really blind?" "No, they see with their ears."

The next day at school we quizzed each other on the same questions. "Which is bigger, the African elephant or the Asian elephant?"

I never remembered the answers. Both elephants looked very big, and since they lived so far apart why start a fight?

The children's show was uncomfortable to watch especially if adults were around. Their lavish praises for the contestants were meant to shame the rest of us into working harder at school. We could not wait until they herded out The Hope of the Future and brought out the real entertainment: the dancing, the music, and the cartoons. But as time went on, bright kids proliferated and monopolized the show, leaving the dim-witted majority with nothing to stare at. But there was one hope. The son of the show's host went to our school.

"Tell him more cartoons and fewer prodigies," we ordered day after day. But the adult lobby was strong, and our inside contact did nothing for us. What sort of a father was he anyway? "Tell him we like the questions, but he should invite normal kids. Right now, the show is for grown-ups."

The son always came back with news that his father believed the programs *were* directed at children. But a few minutes' viewing of the commercials would expose this lie. Kids do not buy shortening, nor can they influence the choice of brand.

At the time, commercials dealt heavily in shortening. It seemed no other industry wished to risk its advertising money on the new medium of television. Even later, as the commercials became more varied and numerous, the shortening commercials determined the state of the art in television advertising. Originally, though, the shortening companies patterned their commercials after Nazi propaganda films. Except that the troops of Nazis were replaced by cans of shortening. Accompanied by glorious Wagnerian music, row after row of handsome and shiny cans rolled off the factory lines displaying proudly the company trademark. As a result, one was left with a subliminal desire to grow up to be a can of shortening. I cannot guess how many of the psychological problems of my generation of Iranians have to do with falling short of this unconscious goal.

It was hard to accept the fact that the son had no pull with his celebrity father. *Our* fathers certainly let *us* tell them how to run their businesses. But what was more frustrating was that the host appeared in our house every day and pontificated on all issues without our being able to tell him anything. Here Iraj tried to be helpful and explained at length that the host was nothing but a complex pattern of blinking lights. Even Iraj's own father, Madani, did not accept this. He had grown up in the village, and despite the ridicule of the city-bred relatives he continued to talk back to the TV. I remember the guffaws he received when he gave morality lectures to the bad guy. I think that is why Iraj's family was the first in the clan to buy a television: it was too embarrassing to take Madani to the movies.

One day after that ungracious pattern of dots had not run cartoons for a very long time, the children at school devised a plan. They would keep the host's son from waiting in front of the school so that the father would be forced to park the car and walk inside to pick up his son. There he would be ambushed and forced to listen.

The son was easy to persuade, and the plan worked beautifully. As the unsuspecting celebrity walked up toward the office to inquire after his son, he was surrounded by a throng of dissatisfied admirers. Seeing him in person was a shocking reality shift, like catching Santa Claus coming down the chimney. Off screen, the host occupied volume and did not grow, shrink, or fade even though he looked redder than ordinary humans. I walked around him, then I jumped up to get a first view of the top of his head. Strangest of all was to see him hear and respond to our noisy questions and demands.

"Sir, ask us a question."

"All right. What is the lightest element?"

"Water."

"Feathers."

"Cork."

It was none of these; there was something lighter still. We kept trying.

"Ashes. Because ashes can blow in the wind."

"Straw. My dad says there is nothing lighter than straw."

"Eyelashes. Except at night when they get heavier."

If the geniuses were here, they would answer right away with something stupid no one had ever heard of and ruin the excitement of the search. There would be no hubbub of consultation. No story-telling.

Finally, someone brought up the cartoon grievance by yelling "Cartoons." He spoke for the whole crowd, because suddenly we picked up the slogan and began chanting "Car toons, car toons, car toons."

The host promised us he would run some cartoons that evening. I walked up and specifically asked for the cartoon where the character dreams of logs being sawed. He agreed cheerfully. Someone else made another demand. The host accepted. Our parting was full of enthusiastic demands and promises.

That evening I gathered as many of my friends and cousins as I could at Iraj's house.

"See, it is not just an empty tube; I talked to him myself in the flesh. I saw the top of his head. He asked us the melting point of ice water. He will play the cartoon with the logs being sawed."

I was so proud. Could Iraj's understanding of antennas and tubes make the television play whatever he wanted? It is not what you know but who you know.

"The shows are taped in advance," Iraj bragged. "He will not play cartoons tonight."

"You will see. He told us. He promised." I did not suspect that once the host's very flesh had made the promise, his image would betray us. Sadly, Iraj was right. The host appeared black and white and elastic as usual. He revealed no recollection of the promise he would make to us in the future. The bright children answered a few questions: "The hardest substance known to man is. . . ." Then the Nazis paraded and our gathering dispersed.

I sat through a few more of his shows hoping he would keep his promise, but there was nothing back there but the Irajian vacuum.

"What is the hardest substance known to man?" a friend asked at school.

"Diamonds," came the brilliant answer.

"Bulletproof vests," countered a sluggish mind.

Vacuum.

Learning is a valued custom with Iranians. Among those who can afford it, few pass up the opportunity for higher education. To date, I have three first cousins with Ph.Ds. Sometimes our admiration for learnedness leads to the attitude that it is not important what we learn, how we learn it, or what use we make of what we know. Hands-on education is not sought after for fear its contents may not be lofty enough. Perhaps the growth of our promising civilization was stunted by our narrow answer to the question, "What is learning?" The richest part of my own education came during our travels across the country. Years later, I continue to learn fresh lessons from these memories. My first trip to the city of Isfahan acquainted me with some of the unacknowledged mythology of Iran. Isfahan had its heyday at a time when, elsewhere, Isaac Newton was discovering the law of universal gravitation.

The Bathhouse of Isfahan

A s we approached Isfahan my parents were having an argument. "It is one thing to punish him for something he has done wrong, quite another to beat him for not doing his homework," my mother said.

"Wrong is wrong," my father argued. "One punishes a child not to retaliate, but to correct—and the fastest way to correct is to let him have it."

"But if it does not work, and it usually doesn't, then after a while it *does* become retaliation. You beat him once to correct him and twice for not responding to your beatings."

"So what do you expect me to do? The boy flunks math and I should praise him for it?" he said.

"He did not flunk math, he just did not get a perfect grade," my mother said angrily.

76

"He didn't do his homework," he said, raising his voice. "If he does his homework, I don't care what grade he gets, as long as it is the best he can do. Why do you encourage mediocrity in him?"

"Because he is not a racehorse. You always. . . ."

"We are entering Isfahan," my father interrupted, shifting gears from father to tour guide.

With its mosques, palaces, bridges, and minarets, Isfahan is the most beautiful city in Iran by unanimous agreement. It became the capital of Persia in 1597, and even though the modern capital, Tehran, has lots of tall buildings, it compares like a rubber ducky to the magnificent swan that is Isfahan.

We were given comfortable quarters on the grounds of the office branch where my father was on business. The grounds were beautifully maintained by the grounds keeper and his wife. There were rose bushes, geraniums, and a fountain pool with red carp in it. In the evenings the grounds keeper rolled up his pants above his knees and dragged out four large water cans from the tool shack. His wife sat at the pool and filled two while he watered the garden with the other two. The flowers rhythmically bowed their heads in gratitude as the water sprinkled over them.

Outside was still more beautiful. The sycamore-lined boulevard traced the banks of the Zayandeh (birth-giver) River. Not far away the ancient Khajou Bridge could be seen still bearing traffic after three centuries. The Isfahanis have a reputation for quick wit—I wonder that they are not credited more for their profound sense of beauty.

The grounds keeper's sons, one my age, the other younger, were appointed to be my guides. They were to confine our sightseeing, however, to within the walls of the grounds. My parents did not think I was old enough to go out in a strange city unsupervised by adults. There was a lot to see: I visited the famous coal bins, the historic tool shack, the amazing kitchen, and the breathtaking chicken coop. We even climbed to the roof (unauthorized) and had a look at the city's minarets, domes, and rooftops. Hamid, the older one, pointed out a pair of minarets.

"Menar Jonboon," he called them, the wiggling minarets. "If you wiggle one of them, the other will also wiggle."

"How do you wiggle a minaret?" I asked.

"A man goes inside and shakes it. Like an earthquake."

"Does it not fall apart?"

"No, it is made of rubber."

That night I complained that I had seen enough of the compound and wished to go and see Menar Jonboon. My mother added her voice to mine and said she wished to see the famous bazaar of Isfahan. My father said he would arrange for a tour.

In the morning a young employee of the office, familiar with the history, geography, and restaurantology of the area, took us in his capable hands. First we went to the notorious all-you-can-eat kabob eatery, where what one eats and how much one pays depends on one's eating and ordering strategy. It was bustling with hungry gamblers. We ate as much as we wanted but we were not able to beat the house out of fair prices.

Back in the car, our guide was telling us about the mysterious bathhouse of Isfahan.

"It was like magic. A single candle heated the water for the entire bathhouse," he said.

"Amazing," said my father. "How is that possible?"

"They say it is thermodynamically impossible, but the ancient engineers found a way."

"How big was the candle?" I asked. It took a few seconds, but he finally indicated a six-inch length with his hands.

"And it never burned out," he added.

"Has anyone tried to figure out how it worked?" my mother asked.

"Yes. European scientists came and looked at it while it was still working. Some said the water was already hot when it passed over the candle, but they checked that out and it was not true. Finally they took it apart to find nothing but a candle and a water tank. Then they put it back together, but it never worked again." We sat in silence, grief-stricken. I would not have believed it anywhere else. But Isfahan is an unsunken Atlantis. And though the magnificent architecture is still intact, the wondrous civilization that built it is in ruins.

"What about the wiggling minarets?" I said. "Did the Europeans tear that apart too?"

78

"Yes," said our guide. My heart sank.

"So its magic was also destroyed?" I asked remorsefully.

"No, they took it apart and found nothing but bricks and mortar, so they put it back together. It still works, though not as well."

"They found no rubber?" I wanted to know.

"No," he laughed.

When we arrived at the minarets, our guide jumped out of the car to negotiate with the ticket seller.

"We are with the government and we would like to see the minarets," he proclaimed.

"You are three adults and one child, and that will be seven tomans," said the ticket seller dutifully.

"They are guests from Tehran; they are with the government."

"The woman and child?"

"The child is only five," our guide lied.

"He looks big enough for marriage," protested the ticket seller.

"Don't be ridiculous, he is only ten."

"You said he was five."

My father and mother came out of the car.

"What is the problem?" my father asked.

"They have raised the ticket prices. We should report this," answered our guide.

"Tell him I know Mr. Mihan," said my father.

"He knows Mr. Mihan, " relayed the guide.

"Who is Mr. Mihan?" the ticket seller asked apprehensively.

"The chief of the Tourist Attraction Agency," said my father.

"Fine," said the ticket seller, disgusted. "You can be Mr. Mihan's guests, but you still have to tip the minaret wiggler."

"How much is the tip?"

"As much as your generosity allows," he said and he hollered for the wiggler.

The wiggler was bent and old. Clearly he had wiggled past his days. He walked as though his body held a referendum at every move. I wondered why he did not sell tickets and let the ticket seller do the wiggling.

"He can't count change," said the ticket seller without being asked.

The wiggler slowly faded into the building to climb the stairs. We waited outside, eyes on the minarets. We knew it would be a long wait.

"Elasticity of material and sympathetic oscillation explains it," my father said.

"It is either rubber or magic," I said.

"If you did your homework, you would not be saying stupid things like that."

"What about the bathhouse, sympathetic oscillations there too?"

"It never existed, just a myth," he said.

"What about the music room in the Ali Ghapoo palace? The musicians played and left, but the music stayed," I insisted.

"Who taught you this nonsense? Ali Ghapoo has good acoustics, but the music does not stay," he stated, looking to our guide for confirmation.

"No one has played there for a long time, but it is believed that the walls act like tape recorders," he said.

"Nonsense," my father concluded as the old man finally appeared in the minaret.

Shakily, he put his palms against the sides and with great effort began to belly dance in that position. For a while he wiggled pathetically with no results, but suddenly, the minaret changed its mind and joined in the dance.

"Look," my mother said excitedly. The minaret was very clearly moving round and round about its base.

"I told you it is magic," I said triumphantly.

"Look, look," said my mother again, pointing at the other minaret. It had also joined in. The three of them, the shaker and his two minarets, were dancing wildly to the music of the creaking brick. And nothing came crashing down.

The old man soon tired and climbed down for his tip. The guide gave him one toman but the old man looked very offended. My father thought this was a good time to test the renowned Isfahani wit.

"Your minarets did not wiggle too well today, " he teased.

The old man, irritated by the pittance he had received for his trouble, indicated a phallus with his forearm and said, "You are used to Tehran rates. Around here you have to pay for a satisfying wiggle."

80

My mother exploded into laughter but quickly controlled it and let my father finish the laugh. My father gave the old man another two tomans for a complaint well put. As we walked out, my mother slipped him another five.

In the morning I told the grounds keeper's sons about the visit to Menar Jonboon. I embellished generously. The younger one, Taghi, wished to know more about the muscle-bound Samson of a minaret shaker who, try as he might, failed to sway the minarets to rubble.

"What was his name?" Taghi asked.

"His name?" I remembered the name we used to get free admission to Menar Jonboon. "His name is Mr. Mihan. Actually, he lives in Tehran and is the head of the tourist office."

"Did you visit the bathhouse too?" the boys asked.

"No, I don't even know where it is. Have you been there?"

"No one has been there since they took it apart—the water is cold," they explained.

"Is it true about the candle only being this big?" I was holding my thumb and forefinger one inch apart.

"Yes, it is true. And it never gets smaller."

"It is magic," I said.

"No, it is a lost science. Our ancestors knew things that no one knows anymore."

We chatted all morning about the ancients, their secret underground tunnel, their flying machines and their healing arts. Around noon, we were interrupted by the boys' mother, who gave Hamid some money to buy their lunch bread. I was invited to go, so I did. It was not wise to ask my parents because I knew permission would not be given.

The first thing we did was cross the street to the river. The Zayandeh was very low this time of year; most of the river bottom was dry and dusty. We climbed over the railing and jumped down to the sediment, forgetting our mission altogether.

"What are we looking for?" I asked.

"Look, a hairpin," came the answer.

"Here's a bottle cap," said Taghi excitedly.

Soon, I found a marvel of my own. It was shiny, whatever it

was, and I had to dig to get it out. Several inches away, I found its partner. Two glass ampules filled with clear liquid.

"What is it?"

"Phials of some sort," I conjectured, scrutinizing my find. The boys started digging around to see if there were any more. They did not find any, so I gave them one of mine.

"I have seen these before," remembered Hamid. "You use a little saw to cut off their heads and then you inject it."

"Let's open them," I said eagerly.

"My mother might not approve," said Hamid.

"Then I will open mine." We found a good rock and carefully broke the tip, spilling the contents all over ourselves. We opened the other one and spilled it too. There was a burning and itching sensation and the skin touched by the liquid turned slightly blue. My nose itched, so I scratched it with a contaminated finger and got some on my face. The boys were having a similar unpleasant experience, so we decided it was time to get the bread and go home.

"I wonder who buried them there," I said on the way to the bakery.

"They must have fallen off a boat when the river was full."

"If they fell off the boat, they would not be so close together, they would drift apart as they sank," I reasoned.

"Maybe they were tied together and the string decayed," said Hamid, defending his boat theory.

"What was in them? Why did it burn?" Taghi asked. No one had a theory.

By the time we bought the bread, we had forgotten about the ampules and were discussing movies. We walked to a theater and looked at the photographs in the showcase. The boys had seen the movie. They told me the entire story, using the photographs as proof. Late afternoon we started for home. As we rounded the last corner, I realized something dreadful awaited me.

My parents were standing at the gate. My mother was crying, my father gritting his teeth. If I were not dead already, he was going to arrange it.

"Don't whip him," my mother said.

82

"He has to be punished. Don't get in the way," said my father angrily.

"Fine, but don't use the belt. It is dangerous. You are too angry right now."

"Five minutes alone with him and he will never go out without permission again," threatened my father. I was cowering behind my mother.

"If you promise not to use the belt," she said.

"All right." He took me inside the bedroom and closed the door. My heart was pounding out of my chest. Then he unbuckled his belt and pulled it out angrily.

"Help, Mother, he is using the belt!" I screamed. He swept the belt across my legs but I skip-roped it and dove behind a chair. He lashed again violently, but the chair caught that one. Suddenly, my mother crashed into the room and stood between me and the belt.

"That's enough, and you better not have hurt him!" she said, looking me over. The places where the mysterious liquid had spilled over my body had become dramatically blue. My mother turned livid.

"Just look at him, you cruel beast! From now on you stop beating him altogether or you will have to deal with me," she growled.

"I did not touch him, just tried to scare him a little." Father sounded confused.

"You call this not touching, you crazy wild man? Look at these bruises!" He looked closely at my skin.

"Did I do that?" he said guiltily. "It did not seem like the belt even touched him." But the evidence was unmistakable.

"You forget yourself when you are angry, like a psychopath. What if you had maimed him? You would be remorseful for the rest of your life. If I let you live that long."

"I had no idea I could lose control like that. I am truly ashamed. You were right about the belt."

But apologies did not suffice: for days his conscience and my mother did not relent.

I never told anyone about the magic phials. Hamid and his brother did not believe in magic; they thought the ampules contained some sort of ancient medicine. The ancestors had possessed truly powerful healing methods. After the treatment, my father did not hit me ever again.

My mother's sense of wonder made her a natural explorer. During our travels she was thrilled by differences and similarities alike. The unexpected was a reassuring confirmation of the inexhaustible variety of the universe, the expected was a revelation of the unity of nature. Her vocal adulation of our discoveries—a new species of flower, a fresh way of making bread, a sameness of attitude toward the in-laws—breathed a warm spirit of adventure into our experiences. She longed to travel outside of Iran. She had spoken to me about India, France, and England. But something or other—money, obligations, illness—always got in the way. Once, she and my father planned a visit to England. I still have the passport picture that she took for that trip, and I still try to pry some answers out of her expression. After that trip fell through, my mother never again mentioned anything about traveling. For reasons still tangled in paradoxes, she chose to go on a different journey.

The Pork Eaters

The runway at the Tehran airport does not run parallel to the visitors' viewing area. After the passengers are boarded, the plane, whistling quietly, trundles out of sight somewhere off to the side of the building. The visitors go back to their chatter while they wait for the metamorphosis to occur. Their conversation is full of travel: "Don't cry, he'll be back before these tears are dry." "On my last trip abroad . . .," ". . . the best restaurant in Beirut . . .," "You know, she's been back from Paris for a month now and she hasn't even called on me once. I guess she's too good for us now that she's seen Europe—she expects me, ten years her elder, to call on *her*." "Do those life jackets on airplanes really help in a crash? I mean if I was falling to the ground and they asked me if I wanted an inner tube or a parachute, I would take the parachute, wouldn't you?"

The sound of glass shivering in the windowpanes alerts the

crowd. Conversations are quickly suspended as a vague tremor swallows the building. A faint rumble quickly becomes an explosive roar as the jet aircraft reemerges—a screaming behemoth pummelling the ground and shaking the air. With a speed unnatural for its bulk, it charges up the runway and leaps into the air, tucking its talons gracefully into its belly. The sun glitters off the bald surface, the air shimmers under the wings: the jet carries away your loved one to a strange land.

The craft leaves in its wake a turbulence of astonishment.

The crowd wonders not the mechanistic, "How do they do that?" but the mystical, "What gods do they worship?" As though in response, the monster quickly becomes a dot in the sky. This dot-making aspect of God's humor is lost on me. Just once, I would like to be amazed by something that is not a tiny dot compared to something else.

My cousin Daryoosh was always more interested than astonished. He believed that the universe could be explained by starting with one plus one makes two. That distant objects appear smaller than the same objects close up carried no omens for him, so it was particularly out of character for him to ask me to say "Haile Selassie" when he found out I was being sent to England on a jet plane.

"Remember," he said, "at exactly seven o'clock, half an hour into the flight, you must say 'Haile Selassie.'"

"Why?" I asked.

"Because at exactly the same moment I will be saying 'Haile Selassie' too."

"Oh."

"Do you understand?"

"I think so, but what does the emperor of Ethiopia have to do with it?"

"Because 'Haile Selassie' is not a common name and it is unlikely that you would want to say it for any other purpose."

I made my promise to him. Several times, I too had felt the same left-on-the-ground feeling after the plane carrying my father had soared into the air. I wish I had thought of asking him to say 'Haile Selassie': it makes the pain of being left behind more bearable.

At five in the morning the Koran was held over the doorjamb

86

and I was passed under it. My aunts and uncles muttered prayers that protect the traveler. Aunt Monavar stuffed a tiny Koran into my coat pocket. I climbed into the lead car with my cousins Daryoosh and Iraj, my brother, my father and Seifpoor, my father's friend and assigned driver. A long caravan of cars loaded with well-wishers bearing pistachios followed us to the airport. It is customary to give pistachios as a going-away present to Europe-bound travelers; it is wisely assumed that pistachios of such high quality will be hard to find outside of Iran.

The road to the airport is paved to impress the foreigner. The shrubbery is maintained American-style with the hedges machined at close tolerances into box shapes. The crickets inhabiting these structures chirp their wistful summer chorus, somewhat resentful of the fact that they are now apartment dwellers. Casting circles of light onto the early morning darkness, fluorescent street lamps arch above our heads like the necks of ruminating brontosauruses.

In the quiet of the car, I am thinking only of the plane ride. Daryoosh is thinking only of the plane ride. Iraj is jealous. Seifpoor keeps checking the rearview mirror to make sure that the motorcade is not breaking up. My father is deep in thought. For the last few months he has been lost in the tempest of anger and guilt that follows a suicide. Is this why I am being sent to England? Ostensibly, there is no one to take care of me after my mother's death, and the English have good boarding schools. But I have overheard Aunt Monavar plead with my father: "Why don't you let him stay with his kid brother at my house until you pull yourself together? It is not good to send a young boy so far away from home, especially if his mother has just died."

It was my mother who was to go to England that summer. My brother and I were to stay with Aunt Monavar while my mother proudly accompanied my father to London, where he was to attend a conference. The British were preparing to pull out of the Persian Gulf islands, and what role Iran would play after the British left was the topic of much dispute.

At first my father anesthetized the pain of guilt by blaming it all on the British. "If they hadn't been such sons of bitches and not toyed with us, the conference wouldn't have been cancelled."

"What do the British have to do with it?" I asked.

"You do not understand these things."

"Tell me anyway."

"I can't. It is secret."

Years later he would be able to tell me. The British, knowing full well that Iran had a territorial claim to the Bahrain islands, had invited a Bahrain representative to the conference. The Iranian representatives, refusing to tacitly acknowledge Bahrain's existence as an independent nation, had pulled out. Did the British think Iranians were that stupid? Did my father think *this* Iranian was so stupid as to believe his mother would commit suicide over a cancelled trip to London? But that morning in the car it seemed to be the going theory, for here I was on my way to London to alleviate a guilt that was based on an insulting misunderstanding of my mother's character.

At the airport, boxes of gift pistachios were crowding all around me. Hugs, "farewell," perfume, cloth, "passport," more hugs, more pistachios, "careful," "write," Koran, "shillings," "airsick," more hugs, more pistachios, "Don't forget 'Haile Selassie.'"

I boarded the plane with my cargo of pistachios. The strangely muffled sounds, the thick, curved ceiling, and the mechanical currents of air made it clear that this space was designed to keep the outside out. The symmetric cabin was cozy and stifling at the same time, betraying the psychology of its makers like a Rorschach. But with the ship operating at forty thousand feet, who would build it any other way? On the other hand, what madness brought them to a place where the bottoms of their feet were higher than any patch of earth?

We taxied to the mysterious spot out of sight of the visitors. There we turned around and, after a moment's hesitation, accelerated to faster than I had ever gone before. I was thinking that, at this speed, we should be running out of runway by now. In response to my thought, the craft left the ground with no theatrics whatsoever. An absence of drama that leaves goose bumps over the flesh.

At this point in the description of a journey, it is traditional to introduce the person sitting next to the storyteller. To be frank, I don't clearly remember who was sitting next to me. All I recall is an annoyed gesture from behind a newspaper when I said "Haile Selassie." I said it several times in quick succession to allow for error in our calculation of simultaneity.

I also performed another experiment of Daryoosh's design. He had asked me to jump up in the air to see if the rear of the craft would hit me in the back. "Why don't I just toss a coin up in the air?" I had suggested. He had agreed to this simplification. Unexpectedly, the coin behaved quite normally, coming back down just where it had gone up. After a pistachio yielded the same uninteresting result, I felt perhaps I *should* try jumping in the aisles. But here my self-consciousness in the presence of fellow travelers left me in default of that debt to science.

We were scheduled to land in Baghdad, but because of a coup that occurred while we were in flight, the Baghdad airport was closed. We made do with a short refueling stop at a military base in some nearby country (Daryoosh insists it must have been Israel, but some of the passengers believed we were in Cairo). Then off to Rome, Frankfurt, and, finally, London.

Two heavily cologned Iranians, friends of my father working at the Iranian embassy in London, helped me through customs. The customs officer let the pistachios go through even though it was clear that he was privately impressed with the tonnage and was sure I was going to open a pistachio store in London. In his official capacity, however, he muttered a bored concern over tobacco and alcohol before lavishly chalking the luggage as cleared. Chalking was the part of the job he enjoyed most thoroughly, and he took Gauguinesque pains to make his work as painterly as possible.

On the way to the boarding school I did notice that the English drove on the wrong side of the road. But, as I later wrote to Daryoosh, since everyone did it wrong, somehow everything worked out right. I had been raised to think of the English as a crafty lot. There is always method to their madness and madness to their methods and they never let you know which is which. There was not a pie in Iran, it was believed, that did not have an English fist in it. They manipulated and manufactured events in Iran for centuries; they were in league with the mullahs; they were in league with the liberals; they were in league with whomever you least suspected they were in league with.

Until the Americans replaced the British as the *deus ex machina* of Iranian politics, the English were considered responsible for every event that took place in the country. The phrase "British Diplomacy" was used to explain anything from the price of chlorine to the color of the city buses.

But I was not raised to hate the British, just to be careful of them. During a visit by my father to London later that year, he heatedly rebuked me for listening to a rash embassy employee who let it be known that he believed the British robbed us of our wealth by tricking or bullying us into unfair oil contracts.

"The oil belongs to whoever can dig it out. We sat on the oil for thousands of years, and no one thought it was worth anything. Now someone shows up who thinks oil has value, he brings in *his* economy, *his* technology, *his* geology, *his* engineering, and *we* want most of the money because we are the ones who have been sitting on it all these centuries. Now tell me, who is being unfair?"

I was not in a position to argue, but my Iranian upbringing immediately made me suspect that the very argument he was using on me was of British manufacture and a manifestation of the dreaded "British Diplomacy." He was sopping wet on one-half of his body because he had been keeping the umbrella mostly over my head. He had a habit of taking me for walks every time he felt I needed to listen to him. If my attention drifted, he would quicken the pace, forcing me to try to keep up with him. While he was talking, a crippled man wearing medals reached out a wet and quivering sleeve for money. My father gave him the worst ignoring from the Iranian arsenal of beggar repellents. I asked why he was so cruel to the beggar. He said he could not be sure that the man did not serve during the Allied occupation of Iran. What a relief, I thought. He hasn't been totally duped yet.

The boarding school building was constructed mainly of brick and composed of several layers of architecture going as far back as Gothic and as far forward as Quonset huts. I was turned over to the schoolma'am. The smell of cologne lingered for a few minutes after the two Iranians left me. When the cologne was gone, I was truly among the British, unprotected, with only my meager life experience of eleven years matched against an ancient empire of duplicity and deceit.

The schoolma'am, Mrs. Cherret, was talking loudly and copiously. I did not understand what she was saying, but I could tell by watching her smiling red cheeks and hearing her motherly inflections that her impression of me was favorable.

How she went on and on. It seemed she was determined to teach me English by saying right there and then everything it was possible to say. The method worked, however; within a few minutes I had reassessed my views on English pronunciation and was beginning to pick the unprinted words raw out of her mouth. At one point she said "food," pronounced "fEawUOeDe" by the English, not "foood" as the Iranian palate simplifies it. I said "yes" in just the way I had heard her say it and thus began my friendship with the English language.

Mrs. Cherret's husband, the schoolmaster, was a hideous old figure who borrowed his mannerisms from school movies of the Gothic variety and purchased his clothes from the set of "Tom Brown's School Days." He wore his black garb with such ferocious scholarship that the rest of him mysteriously vanished in an aura of sublime learnedness. His was truly the cloak of invisibility inside which he could squelch the light of his humanity and pursue with cold detachment the brutal task of implanting an education beneath the stubborn crania of the wretched ignorentsia entrusted to his mercy. The boys feared him with a terror reserved for spirits, shadows, and dentists.

Mrs. Cherret took me to his office to introduce me. Mr. Cherret looked up a few minutes after we had entered the room and scanned my face, coldly collecting the minimum visual information necessary to identify me. He asked my name to provide a label for this data and dismissed me to join the other boys in the rec room.

In the rec room, an older boy named Howard approached me and made me feel at home by teaching me to play pool. Once I was used to him teaching me things, he began to socialize me in the ways of the English. What is polite and how shoes are polished. Why we wear white shirts on Sundays and grey shirts the rest of the week. When to wear the cap and when to remove it. How to ask for seconds and who can tell whom what to do. Howard was gentle, with a patient, even voice. He was not overly friendly with anyone; he had no pals. But he treated everyone with great consideration. He was lonely in a natural and happy way. I had not seen anyone like him in Iran, but during my year's stay in England I would meet more people like him. Clearly, this climate grew a crop that did not exist back home. And it was easy to see that the reverse was also true.

The first night was the hardest. I shared a dormitory room with four other boys: Gill, an orthodox Hindu; McConekie, with freckles and a nasal voice; Erikson, a fair-haired, blue-eyed New Zealander with a ski-slope nose; and Rusty, whose real name was Rastegarmanesh. He was the other Iranian in the school. I was a year younger than the other boys and would have normally slept in another room with my age group. But they must have thought I would feel more comfortable sleeping in the same room as Rusty. They were wrong. Rusty and I got along marginally. He acted entirely too anglicized to be taken seriously as a compatriot. He did ask me, in broken Farsi, if I had brought any pistachios. I told him that I had brought all of them and that I did not think there were any left in Iran. He stared for a moment and then asked if he could have some.

Rusty was Iranian in one major respect, however: on the pain of death he would not eat pork. He had barricaded all of his Iranianness into this one last rampart which he defended like an Alamo. It was as though he felt that if he ate pork, the last bit of Iranian in him would disappear, leaving behind nothing but an Englishman. Moreover, he had made it his mission to protect all his countrymen within his reach from this evil meat that had the power to gulp down one's heritage with one swallow. Under Rusty's watchful priesthood, and much to the irritation of Mrs. Cherret, who sat at our table, I also maintained my chastity against pork.

Despite this omission, I would have still eaten a balanced meal if Gill, the Hindu, had not been giving sermons at night as to the perils of beef. With Gill's spiritual guidance I also succeeded in avoiding the corruption of beef. Mrs. Cherret was becoming quite irked with me. Rusty and Gill were respected as their abstinence stemmed from moral conviction, but there was no question of conviction on my part: I was clearly being too impressionable.

"Dear," Mrs. Cherret would say, "if you stopped eating whatever someone else didn't eat, you would go hungry." Nevertheless, before every meal, I would ask her whether it was beef or pork. Speaking softly so Mr. Cherret at the next table could not hear, she would say, "It is dog, dear, so you can go ahead and eat it."

While Rusty and I did not quite become friends, Erikson and I became enemies. The first night at the dorm I woke up to his sobbing. I asked him what the matter was. He said he wanted his mommy. This was a very different Erikson than I had met earlier in the rec room. There, social and confident, he was bragging about his girl-friends back in New Zealand. I was not sure if he was really awake now. I told him, as well as I could, that my mother had recently died. He said he was sorry and stopped sobbing.

The next morning he seemed unaware of our conversation the night before and was his bragging self again. That night, after the lights went out, I asked him if he still missed being away from home. He said he missed having sex with his girlfriends. McConekie's ears pricked at this and he started asking for sex advice from Erikson. It became customary that after Gill's sermon against beef, Erikson would open the floor to sex questions. His advice consisted mainly of the citing of precedent, using his own exploits as examples of correct sexual behavior. Rusty sometimes challenged Erikson's credibility and was challenged back.

"How would you know, Rusty? You don't even have girlfriends in Iran."

"Yes we do. Isn't that right?"

"It is true," I would confirm.

"Yes, but they are not common like in New Zealand."

"Persian girlfriends are famous for being common. Isn't that right?"

I nodded and thought, I lied for you, countryman. Someday I may need you to lie for me in this strange land.

"Gill, do you have girlfriends in India?" Erikson asked. Gill was in deep REM, his exhortations against beef having exhausted him.

"Gill . . . , Giiilllll . . . , wake up," Erikson insisted. Finally, he crawled over and shook him awake. Gill sat up puffy-eyed and puzzled.

"Gill, do you have girlfriends in India? We are all curious."

"No," Gill explained and pulled the blankets over his head.

I tried several times to get Erikson to talk about missing his mother, but instead he started acting rudely toward me. He nick-named me "shrimp." Since he had a slight seniority over me, I could not challenge what he chose to call me. Soon all his friends were calling me shrimp.

The seniority concept was hard for me to grasp. It was the Great Loophole in the ideals of justice and fair play we were being taught to uphold. Seniority capitalized Bully and underlined force; it put (ethics) in parentheses and placed "fair play" in quotes. Later in my education I would recognize its relatives in the texts of two centuries of Iran-British treaties in which pages of acceptably balanced give-and-take would be rendered totally meaningless by a single clause overriding all that went before. It would drag its muddy feet into America, where an entire profession is devoted to discovering in-tended or unintended loopholes so that the discoverer can cheat openly without breaking the law.

Erikson soon became relentless in his needling, taking every op-portunity to jab at me. I would find pencil shavings in my socks and mud on my toothbrush—and Erikson and his advisees always smirking and giggling within sight. Rusty sat the fence on this issue. McConekie went over to Erikson's camp. Gill was on my side, always rebuking Erikson for acting spoiled. Since Gill had the same seniority as Erikson, his rebuke went much further than my frustrated squeaks. But still Erikson continued his heckling.

I complained to Mrs. Cherret. She said, "Isn't Howard watching out for you?" I told her I had already talked to Howard about it.

"What did he say?"

"He said, 'Well, what are you going to do about it?'"

"What *are* you going to do about it?" she asked.

"I have complained to Howard, I have complained to all the bishops (English school monitors). I don't know who else to talk to who will believe me. Maybe next time I go to the embassy I can talk to someone there, or maybe I should write a letter to my father."

That day at the lunch table, Erikson passed me a note. I opened it. It said, "Hello Shrimp." I saw my opportunity and immediately showed the note to Mrs. Cherret. She did not put her fork down but said coolly, "Erikson, we do not pass notes at the table." This was truly frightening. I had caught him red-handed in his cruelty, fully expecting he would be dismissed from the table and punished. Instead, English authority seemed not a bit concerned.

The needlings continued until I finally had the chance to talk to Mr. Cherret about it. Erikson and his gang had taken away my ball and were playing "keep away." I was jumping and yelling to try to get my ball back. Hubble, the extremely tall, most senior of the bishops, heard the commotion and came over to investigate. Hubble was difficult to read; his face had been chiseled in ice and hardly moved. It was reputed that if one were brave enough to look carefully into his deep blue eyes, one would see the cross hairs of a rifle scope. He took my ball away from the Erikson gang but did not give it back to me. I asked him where he was going with my ball. He told me in his stilted fashion that the ball had been confiscated. I did not know what "confiscated" meant and wondered what had happened to my ball. Later, I asked Hubble about it. He said Mr. Cherret had it and I could go see him about it. I would lose a hundred balls before I would see Mr. Cherret about anything, but here was my chance to take my complaint to the highest authority of all. The next day, early in the morning, I knocked timidly on his door. My stomach was a vacuum, my legs were rubber. His voice told me to go in.

I walked into the oak and leather chamber. Mr. Cherret was at the bookshelves. My small rubber ball was centered on his bare desktop. British Diplomacy, I thought.

"What is it?" he probed.

"Sir, Erikson took away my ball and. . . . " I could see by his annoyed expression that he did not wish me to continue to whine my petty complaint to him. " . . . and Hubble took it."

"Hubble took your ball?" he said.

"No, sir, he . . . he did something to it." I could not remember "confiscate."

"What did he do to it?"

"He . . . he confused it sir."

"Hubble confused your ball?" His interest was waxing.

"No, sir, he . . . he confessed it, sir."

"Why would he do that?"

"I don't know, sir, he just confessed it and when I asked him, he said it had been confessed and that I should see you about it."

"You have done as he asked. You may go to your class now." I
hesitated for a moment to see if he would give me the ball. He went
back to the bookshelf. Did he expect me to just take the ball? That
would have been terribly impolite by Iranian standards. Confused, I
walked out of the office. It seemed I was doomed to live under
Erikson's tyranny forever. Disappointed and disheartened, I knew now
that talking to Mr. Cherret was a mistake. While I had hope, I could
bear the torment, but now that everything had failed me, I would
certainly break down.

The breakdown happened one suppertime when Erikson made a
face at me. I banged my fists on the table, weeping. I wanted to call
him something vile, but I could not think of anything vile enough
that would not make him smirk even worse. The boys in the dining
room stared aghast at my behavior. Rusty looked embarrassed, but he
gave me what I needed: I turned to Erikson and spat out venomously,
"Pork eater, pork eater, pork eater!" Erikson was taken aback. His
smirk disappeared. "Pork eater, pork eater!" I yelled, but the surprise
was beginning to wear off. The smirk reappeared. I stomped out of the
dining room without being dismissed. Mr. Cherret looked up briefly,
then went back to his potatoes.

That night there was silence in the dormitory. No one wished
to talk about what had happened at dinner. We all feared that if we
talked about anything at all, we might end up discussing my blowup.
This lasted a few days. What had been a small silliness between two
boys was now a schoolwide scandal with Erikson as the hero and with
me as the crybaby. Erikson's fans were ever more devoted to him, and
my friends, even Gill and Howard, were cooler toward me. Rusty was
still fence-sitting. But things would change.

We were all sitting in the rec room watching television. Badu
from Nigeria and Zia from Pakistan were playing pool. Charles, Badu's
much younger brother, was asking Hubble's permission to play pool
after the seniors were done with their game. Hubble seemed amused,
as Charles had to stand on a chair to gain the necessary height. Except
for the chair, Charles was not a bad pool player. Rusty and Erikson
were arguing over girlfriends again. I overheard Erikson say, "Persian
girlfriends grow up to be ugly-looking women." I had heard him belittle Persian women for a long time without reacting, but now I felt a

rush of anger. I didn't care how many friends he had, how much older he was, what seniority he had, what Mr. Cherret would do, or what England would do to Iran as a result. I would draw the line in blood if I had to. I walked over, stood very close to him and said, "My mother was a Persian woman and she was beautiful."

Erikson's face dropped. He momentarily lost his smugness, but before he could recover and start laughing again, I grabbed him by the collar, lifted him out of his chair, and pushed him back into it again. He went tumbling backward, chair and all.

In Iran, the unspoken rules of the fight dictate the following sequence: A hits B; B is allowed to hit back once; then half the rest of the alphabet grabs a struggling A and the other half grabs a struggling B and urges the feuding parties to make up. This sequence is not honored in England. There, the battle is to the death, and may the best man live.

There was a delayed roar of excitement. Like an atomic blast, first the intense flash, the shock, the power, and then the thunder. Erikson bounced up, somewhat shook up but ready to fight. He tore off his jacket with the school emblem on it and handed it to McConekie. I tore off my jacket and looked for a volunteer to hold it. There was a hesitation, then Hubble stepped in proudly and took it. Another roar as the fight was sanctioned by authority.

Unknowingly, I had pressed a button that had invoked the ancient traditions of these people. Quickly, the area was cleared and the ritual circle was formed. Tactical advice began pouring in noisily from all sides. "His leg, his leg, grab his leg." "Watch that elbow." "Keep it coming." "Don't look into his eyes."

Erikson and I tangled furiously, the circle widening and narrowing with the convulsive rhythm of our battling. He growled and leaped at me like a tiger. We fell to the floor rolling and jabbing. Persians are by genetic stock good wrestlers. Freestyle wrestling is one of our fortes in the Olympics. I found that while on the floor, I could quickly tangle him up and gain the advantage. He saw that he could fight better standing up as he was taller and more accustomed to the use of his fists. Iranians regard punching as unsportsmanlike. It revolted me to see him fight so unfairly. Our differences were so deep, we could not even agree on how to fight.

"Don't punch, you coward. How would you like it if I bit and scratched?"

Confused, Erikson responded with a quick left hook which I narrowly ducked. The next hook caught me in the mouth. It sent me reeling backward, my head stuffed with cotton candy. "All right, if you want to fight like an animal, I will fight you like an animal," I thought, as I reeled back into the pool table and fell face down onto the felt. Colors and stripes went flying. Erikson was rushing over to finish me off. He would twist my arm behind my back and make me eat the eight ball, but, unfortunately for him, my donkey senses had been awakened.

I had grown up with donkeys. Vendors selling salt, onions, fruits, and such carried their wares on donkey back. It was important for the Iranian in his day-to-day life to know where not to stand while making a purchase. My long-eared compatriots had mysteriously taught me exactly what I needed to know in this moment of crisis: without being able to see, I knew exactly where Erikson was relative to my hooves. At the right moment, I tucked my legs into my body as though loading a charge and, hoisting myself up on the pool table like a gymnast, I sprang straight with all my strength.

When I looked back, Erikson was still in the air, his trajectory targeting the rack of billiard cues at the far end of the room. He fell with a crash that would shame a Hollywood stuntman. The crowd did not know what to make of this maneuver. It looked like kicking, which is dishonorable; on the other hand, it was no ordinary kick that had launched Erikson into such a graceful parabola. "Persian judo!" Rusty cried exultantly, and the rest were noisily impressed. Some even began immediate practice. Given a name with a tradition behind it, my dirty trick was now a hallowed form of martial arts. We Iranians stuck together, didn't we, Rusty?

Erikson sat stunned, knocked out once by the mule kick and again by Rusty's apotheosis of it. He scrambled up pitifully, billiard cues falling like quills off an injured hedgehog. I could read his mind. What a fool he had been to fall for my whining pretense. He was merely being led to the slaughter. Since it was his mother's sincere wish that he complete his education in the northern hemisphere, it did not seem prudent to tangle further with this Iranian that could send him back to New Zealand with one kick.

I went to finish him off with a few ritual bashings. His resistance was puny. He even began to whimper. I was going to stop and call it a day when all of a sudden his eyes glazed and he stopped responding to my blows. Not falling for that old trick, I pummelled him some more. But he hung unresisting like a punch bag. I looked up guiltily at the crowd to see if they thought I had killed him, but the same transformation had come over them. They all stood with glassy eyes focused at a point behind me. Slowly, I turned around.

Behind me stood Mr. Cherret, fully cloaked in his black garb. He stood silently like a tall afternoon shadow. He held a cane partly in his sleeve. Then he said with dreadful calmness, "The office in five minutes." He looked at his watch and left. He did not say *who* in the office in five minutes. We were to supply the details ourselves. Cherret was a calculating man, well steeped in the traditions of "British Diplomacy." If he did not intend to use the cane until "the office in five minutes," why did he bring it along? Was he giving pain time to prepare itself? Pretty itself up so that when it finally came, it would be memorable?

Soon after he left, the crowd animated like a stopped movie frame rolling back to life. Erikson and I were being coached on how to avoid the worst of the pain. "Cold water." "Hot water." "Think brick." Five minutes later, Erikson, Hubble, and I sorrowfully trudged up to Golgotha.

At the office, Mr. Cherret angrily nodded Hubble to a seat. Mr. Cherret never became angry in front of the boys. This was staged. He picked up his switch and beckoned Erikson and me to follow him. He took us to the sideyard in front of the locker room where our jumping up and down and thrashing about would not break anything. A quick slice of the whip across the fingertips, then he left us. At first there was a numb message to the brain that something had gone wrong in the vicinity of the arms. He had placed his whip exactly where the nerve endings are the most populous so that when the shock wore off, the maximum number of pain messages would be sent. We held our fingers between our legs and howled as we skipped about, trying to shake off the pain. While we pogo-sticked, I noticed that Erikson was trying to tell me something.

Hoarsely, with sheets of pain slicing over his teary, red eyes, he said, "Are you all right?"

Suddenly, my heart reached for him, making my tears run even faster. "Yes, are you?"

"Bloody hurts," he smiled.

Erikson and I became the best of friends. Cracking pistachios, we discussed our families to our heart's content, making that year in England one of the happiest of my life. In the summer, we all went home. I told Mrs. Cherret that I would be coming back next year and that she should pack only my summer clothes. She said, "Are you sure?"

"Positive," I said.

She suggested maybe she should at least pack my winter socks. I assured her I was coming back.

The BOAC craft came in for a night landing on a beautifully lit Tehran. Dozens of my relatives were noisily waving at me from the visitors' area. I waved back happily. Daryoosh was most enthusiastic in his huggings. As I was bounced and hugged and loved, I saw a child's face in the crowd. How could I have forgotten him? He could not write and I had not asked about him. As he caught my eyes I knew why. Suddenly, a year of blocked emotions burst to the surface. I rushed over and picked up my kid brother and hugged him and hugged him and hugged him, knowing that I had missed him so deeply that I would not have been able to bear it if I had remembered him.

I never went back to England. Life would lead me elsewhere. Mrs. Cherret must have known that, for when I unpacked my suitcase, I noticed my winter socks had been packed, rolled into each other. One of the rolls was much bigger than the others. Curiously, I opened it and found tucked inside the ball that had been confessed.

Friends at the Iranian embassy in London sometimes took me to the embassy cultural events. It was good to stay in touch with home, if only to speak Farsi for a few hours. The embassy itself was a source of cultural surprises, each profession and institution bearing its own traditions. On one occasion I ran into a way of life more distant than any I had seen before: the ruling-class culture of my own country.

The Ambassador

When Hatefi came to get me at the boarding school, he was greatly excited.

"Put on your best clothes and your best shoes. We are going to an embassy party," he said excitedly.

"What is the occasion?" I asked, rushing to get ready.

"What is the occasion? What is the occasion? A few months in England and the boy forgets everything. It is Nowrooz!" he shouted. "You remember what that is, don't you?"

"Really!" I jumped with joy. "It is Nowrooz already?"

"Happy New Year," he said and gave me the ceremonial kisses on the cheek. This was the coldest Nowrooz I had ever seen. It was the first day of spring, but London was still in winter.

"Never mind the weather. We'll do the best we can," he said, as he drove crazily to the embassy. "Do you know the ambassador? He

102

is the Shah's son-in-law, a very nice man, no pretensions, one of us. You will meet him. When you do, be very polite, but don't be shy. He hates shy kids."

Hatefi was an assistant to one of my father's friends who worked at the embassy. He had been told to look after me, and he did so with great kindness. He also enjoyed taking time off from the office to take me and himself sightseeing. He liked to talk, and instructing me in the ways of the world gave him a good excuse.

We arrived at the embassy and walked up to the reception hall, the rumble of party chatter all around us. The ambassador was at the entrance, greeting the guests. I had seen his picture in the newspapers and thought he had charisma: seeing him in person confirmed my impression. I felt at home just looking at him.

"The Shah's son-in-law," Hatefi reminded me. We walked up; the ambassador noticed Hatefi.

"Happy New Year, Hatefi," he said cordially.

"Happy New Year, sir," Hatefi answered.

"Your son?" queried the ambassador, scruffing my hair.

"No sir, I am just looking after him."

"Good man to look after anybody," the ambassador assured me. Then he reached into the huge silver bowl next to him and pulled out a fistful of *noghl* (candy-coated nuts) mixed with newly minted Persian coins and stuffed it in my pocket. "Welcome. Go inside and enjoy yourselves," he said as he noticed some other guest in need of attention. He gave Hatefi a pat on the back and reached out to greet the new guest.

"Nice man," Hatefi said, craning his neck around, looking for something. Suddenly he found it and whisked me in its direction.

"Caviar. Have you ever had caviar?" he asked as he pushed me through the crowd like an upright vacuum cleaner.

"Fish eggs?" I asked.

"No, that is *khaviyeh*. Caviar is fish eggs too, but see if you can tell the difference." There was a giant crystal vat that contained what looked like an oil spill. Emerging from this swamp and rising prominently above it were muddy mounds of black magma. Hatefi scooped up some of the contents with the silver spoon and slathered it on a wafer. "Here, eat this," he said as he helped himself to the mound.

"Thank you," I said politely and started nibbling on the lightly salted fish eggs. It was good so I threw the whole wafer in my mouth.

"You like it," Hatefi said. "Very sensible of you. The best caviar in the world comes from the Iranian Caspian. Here, let me make you a sandwich." He selected two pieces of toast and mortared them together with an inch of caviar and offered it to me proudly. "If anyone tells you the Russians have the best caviar, send them to me. The best sturgeon swim to our side of the sea, too much industrial pollution on their side. Actually, there is no 'their side'; the Caspian is all ours. The bastard Russians bullied us out of most of it. You know the treaty they made us sign says we can't even have a navy there?"

"Mmmmph?" I mmmphed.

"Really good stuff. It is beluga caviar. More?" I wanted to say I had had enough but I needed to swallow before I could talk. By then he had stuffed another in my mouth. "You will never see this much caviar again, I promise you . . . unless you work in the factory!" He laughed, looking around. The guests were busy chatting and eating. Hatefi pointed out the other food tables.

"All that dried fruit, wonderful stuff. Iran is a major exporter of dried fruits and nuts. Peaches, mulberries, pistachios, raisins. Look at this wealth. Do you know how many different kinds of grapes we grow?" He waited for an answer. I counted four. "Two hundred. Can you believe that?"

"No, that is too many," I said.

"And that is just the grapes." We walked over to the platters of dried fruits and nuts. "Dried cherries, almonds, walnuts. We should try them all with caviar, don't you think?" I told him I thought walnuts might agree with caviar, but dried cherries are best eaten without fish eggs. "Go ahead, make fun, but Iran has the best agriculture in the world. This new agriculture that they do here—it makes a cherry as big as an apple, but it tastes like sawdust. If you want fruit that tastes like fruit, eat Iranian fruit."

"I was not making fun. I just think caviar is better without anything with it," I said.

"You have to try it with butter. I will prove you wrong." We went back to the caviar swamp, where he paved a piece of toast with butter, only to bury it under a mudslide of caviar. "Try this if you think caviar is good by itself."

"Please, no more caviar," I protested, but he looked boyishly disappointed. He so wanted to prove me wrong.

"All right," I said. "Let me try it." He was right. I admitted my error.

"You know Americans eat peanut butter with jelly," he said with a nauseated expression.

"So do the English. It is worse than caviar and dried cherries."

"Much worse. The English learned it from the Americans. The ambassador used to be ambassador to America, did you know that?"

"No. What is he doing here?"

"He is too pro-Republican. While a Democrat is in office, he is in hiding."

The ambassador was now surrounded by an admiring group of listeners. Suddenly they all started laughing. He raised his hand to indicate he was not finished yet, then he uttered a few more sentences. This time the crowd exploded into guffaws. Meanwhile, Hatefi had built me another caviar sculpture, this one fortified with lime juice.

"Hatefi, I really can't. You don't want me to throw up in front of the Shah's son-in-law, do you?" Hatefi retracted the monument but immediately offered it again.

"Don't throw up," he ordered. "The best lime in the world. Iranian. Comes from the northern regions." Then he dipped his head in the direction of the ambassador and whispered, "But if his father-in-law has his way, we are going to end up *importing* food."

"Why?" I asked.

"Shhht, tell you later."

By the time the party wound down, I felt like a pregnant sturgeon. Hatefi's assurances that sturgeon do not become pregnant did not help.

"Don't fill up on caviar," he said. "After the party a few of us are going to the private quarters to have tea and sweets."

"Hatefi, you have fed me too well. I cannot eat any more."

"Eat. Nowrooz comes once a year."

When the party ended, a few of the guests went to the private quarters and waited for the ambassador. His young daughter, the Shah's beloved grandchild, was playing in the curtains, threatening to bring them down. Her nanny looked very stressed. She could not scold the child, but she would be held accountable for anything the princess destroyed. The girl swam through the curtains and began yanking on the tablecloth. We all held our breaths and prayed she would not pull all the food off the table. Hatefi spotted a small dish with a mound of gold caviar on it.

"Royal caviar," he said, awestruck and salivating. "Extremely rare. Reserved for the royal family. We must rescue it before the carpet eats it."

"If you hadn't fed me all that black caviar, I would have room," I chided.

"Let's go have a spoonful anyway."

"You go, I will watch."

"You will not find this in stores, even if you could afford it. You will be sorry. You don't have to swallow it, just taste it." He fed me some yellow caviar and made me swallow it. It would have been a waste to throw up royal caviar. I did not puke out of frugality.

Her highness was now pulling the drawers out of the oaken desk and slamming them shut. She had already tipped some chairs over and the table setting was clearly askew. Finally, the ambassador showed up and, noticing the condition of the room, ordered the nanny to take the child to the zoo.

Good, I thought. Throw her in a cage and put a "do not feed" sign on her. It was further decided that the child should choose one of the children present to accompany her in case the animals did not prove sufficiently entertaining.

Me, me, me, I thought. I desperately needed a "do not feed" sign. The princess looked me over and seemed interested, but I lost her to another boy who did not reek as badly of fish eggs.

"Your caviar ruined me, Hatefi," I whispered.

"That is all right. You should not get mixed up with royalty anyway. Just think, you might have to eat caviar every day."

"I would abdicate my throne to avoid caviar," I asserted.

The ambassador sat on the ornate oaken desk dangling his legs.

He had loosened his tie and collar and was issuing short directives to his aides. He was handed a tin box by one of them, and he asked for a can opener. Everyone started a body search for one. I told Hatefi that I was carrying a pocketknife that had a can opener on it.

"Why don't you offer it?" he asked.

"Because I don't want to have to eat whatever is in that box. I am getting sick."

"Don't get sick," he said.

Finally someone came up with the can opener, but the box was too hard to open. The ambassador nicked his finger on the sharp metal. He did not seem particularly concerned, but his aides were rushing about trying to come up with a Band-Aid. While the finger was being bandaged, the ambassador said, "The Turks have found a good way to package their dried fruit. They seal it in plastic and stuff the bag in a cardboard box. Really easy to open. We have been using the same tin-can-and-solder method for years—when is Iran going to become enterprising?"

There was a rumble of consensus. I was shocked. I had heard this Iran-bashing a lot but assumed it had to do with people being displeased with the leadership. I did not expect to hear it from so high up. Surely if anyone was to feel responsible for correcting the ills of Iran, it was people like him.

On the way back to the boarding school I sat bloated in the car. Hatefi had the same reaction to the ambassador's statement and was giving me a political lecture.

"You see, people are looking for leaders to inspire them, and leaders are looking for inspired people to lead. Deadlock. Like two cats in a stare-down. Meanwhile the world is passing us by. These industrial enterprises we have going are worthless. It looks like technology, but all we do is assemble the parts made elsewhere. We just tighten the screws. Is that industry?"

"No," I said.

"And all that lovely food on the table—we are losing it fast. Agriculture is being destroyed by this so-called land reform. The farmers are all coming to the city to tighten screws. So we will import, you say. But when the oil runs out, what are we going to eat then, huh? What are we going to eat then?"

My stomach growled in alarm. "What's wrong with caviar?" I burped.

I returned from England to a new way of life. We sold the big house in the desert suburb and moved in with Aunt Monavar. When my brother was a little older, we bought our own house in the city near where my father worked. Relatives and friends continued to introduce my father to eligible women, and our circle of friends expanded to include these women, but contrary to the Iranian norm, my father refused to marry again. With some help from Monavar and Tooran, he took on my brother's care himself and hired a manservant to do the housework.

I was not yet thirteen, but I had traveled far. At gatherings, adults earnestly sought me out to discuss travel. It did not matter that my opinions were immature; my listeners made allowances. In the spirit of Hatefi's ramblings, friends told me about Nassereddin Shah, the king who, in my grandfather's time, visited Europe. His famous travelogue is often cited by Iranians as an example of the naiveté with which the Iranian ruling class encountered Imperial Europe. I heard many lamentations over our loss of wealth and territory. After the loss of my mother, grief came easily, and I remember being heartbroken by these stories. Vacations on the Caspian shore were always colored by the knowledge that much of our heritage now lies on the stern side of Soviet gunboats.

The Tunnel

The hardest part about going to the beach with the Kazemis was having to wake up at four in the morning. This was quite unnecessary. We were never on the road before midmorning anyway. Always, at the last minute, Kazemi would attempt some minor improvement on his car. The spare needed fixing or the brake lights were failing or the old generator belt was suspicious. Swaying like a mast in the wind, I would stand half-asleep, wondering why he could not do his repairs while I slept.

It was an unconscious ritual Kazemi and my father performed every so often. It reminded them of the times during World War II when they spent the predawn hours rigging their explosives-laden truck in preparation for the haul. It was important that nothing fall off. My father was once almost executed for delivering short. He was tried by the Russians for theft of war supplies, but the evidence suggested the rigging had failed. They just gave him a beating for being careless. Such happy endings need to be commemorated.

We would be traveling the same road across the Alborz Range, so no one should sleep while they reenacted the drama of their war days. Kazemi was not satisfied with the mere pretense of wakefulness. He rolled down the car windows all the way to let in the tornado. After that, we in the back seat—Kazemi's son, my brother and I—sat up cheerfully, letting the wind slap our clothes around our bodies.

The trip through the industrialized desert of west Tehran was uninspiring. My father and Kazemi discussed the real estate potential of the scenery. But as soon as we reached the Karaj River and headed north through the mountains, a canopy of giant trees engulfed us in its spiritual shadow, and quickly the value of real estate dropped.

"The private road," declared my father, begging a question.

"Why do they call it private?" I asked.

Kazemi answered. "That is the old name for it. It used to be only the Shah could use it. Not this Shah. The old Shah, his father."

"Is that why it is only wide enough for one car?" A car coming from the other direction almost scraped us.

"Actually, it is wide enough for trucks," my father reminded me.

"Did the old Shah own trucks?" Kazemi's son, Hojjat, joined in.

"No," said Kazemi. "They probably had other things in mind when they built it. Just like the railroad."

He meant the trans-Iranian railroad built by the Germans and the Italians. History books laud it as the old Shah's greatest accomplishment, a giant step toward building a modern nation. Many years' earnings of a poor nation went into this project, the immediate reward of which was the Allied invasion of Iran. The Persian Gulf and the Caspian Sea had to be connected by railroad, not because of the economic needs of Iran but because of the strategic needs of the West. As it turned out, the British used the railroad to supply the Russians against the Germans. Alternatively, the Germans would have used it for their own plans against Russia. This major blunder of which old Reza Shah was so proud may explain the persistence of the many apocrypha attesting to his stupidity.

As we wound our way up the mountains, the Karaj Dam came

The Tunnel

into view. The blue of the dam lake seemed out of place in these barren elevations. This reminded Kazemi of a story.

"One day Reza Shah went to visit a dam. The engineer explained to him that water is used to make electricity. Reza Shah rebuked the engineer and had him fired. Later he explained that in a country as arid as Iran, no one has any business converting precious water to electricity."

"It is possible that he may not have had any choice in the matter," my father said, referring back to the railroad business. "Reza Shah was quite a nationalist, and what they say about his being illiterate and stupid is not true. Leaders of nations like ours work with limitations. They are not entirely masters in their own house. Even today our development is linked to the interests of the West. They allow no other sort of development."

But my mind was beginning to wander from the discussion. The tree line was now hundreds of feet below us. Already the scale of the architecture was playing tricks with the perception of distance. Things were a lot further away than they looked, and the distant past seemed so much closer. I was searching the monstrous rocks for our mythical past, hoping to find Zohaak's skeleton. I would be able to recognize it among other skeletons I might find, as it had two snakes growing out of its shoulders.

The evil Zohaak usurped the throne of good King Jamshid. Jamshid, who taught us how to weave, heal and build, grew complacent and arrogant in his last days and was defeated by Zohaak, the first meat eater. The villain was overthrown in a popular uprising. If legend can be believed, he was chained to these very rocks.

"All the Earth was once the bottom of an ocean. Can you believe that?" Kazemi interrupted my thoughts. He had been following another path through the mountains into faraway times.

"Do they know where Zohaak is chained?" I asked.

"No, but it is supposedly somewhere around Mount Demavand, to the east of here."

My brother, who had been nagging about breakfast all morning, was scanning the valley far below for signs of water. Maybe there was a teahouse hidden down in that cluster of trees hugging that stream.

111

"I'm hungry," he moaned.

"Do you know how Zohaak got his snakes? It was because he liked to eat so much," my father warned. "The demon Eblis came to him disguised as a chef and prepared such delicious meat dishes that Zohaak was overwhelmed and asked the chef to name his reward. Eblis asked only to be allowed to kiss the king's shoulders. Where he kissed, snakes grew out."

"Did the snakes eat him?" asked my brother, forgetting his hunger.

"He had them cut off, but immediately new ones grew. They threatened to eat him. None of his healers could help. At last Eblis appeared, this time as a healer, and told him the snakes would be appeased if they were fed human brains. So he sacrificed two men a day until the people rose against him."

"Did they eat him after he was chained to the mountains?" my brother asked.

"The story does not say," said my father.

"Was this place under an ocean in those times?" my brother wondered.

Kazemi laughed. "No, Zohaak is just a legend."

No story about the Alborz Range is just a legend. This is a natural place of worship and contemplation. Islam works hard to sway the mind toward the desolate abstractness of God. It succeeds in the city, but here among the gigantic idols carved by Earth herself Allah gives way to the solid sacredness of rocks. No book or message extracts such worship. Perhaps faith moves mountains, but surely mountains move us to faith.

My paganistic heresy was interrupted by a ghastly sight. The shattered carcass of an automobile had been put on display on the side of the road—a warning to drivers to slow down. But to the pilgrim in the mountains the warning was just another reminder that we were mortals. So the first message was lost, and most people drove as though touching the brake pedal counted against them on Judgment Day.

A few vicious curves later, upturned in the riverbed was the red convertible that had passed us in a suicidal hurry. Kazemi had heaped curses upon the driver; now he was sorry and mumbled a short prayer for the departed. I told him that my uncle, the veterinarian, had plunged off the cliffs twice; both times he had survived and his passengers died. As I related this, another car, inspired by the fate of the red convertible, passed us on a blind curve. There was a terrible sound of tires screeching and horns honking as the passing car cut in front of us to avoid an oncoming car. More curses. The offending driver was angry at us for being so slow he had to pass.

"My condolences to his mother," Kazemi said.

Halfway through the trip, we reached a congestion. The serpentine road had developed a shoulder. There were cars pulled over waiting.

"The Kandovan Tunnel," Kazemi proclaimed with great awe.

We slowed to a stop behind the long line of waiting cars. The air was cold. The cliffs were shading us and a dripping sound echoed all around. The mountain, immovable, was standing in the way, telling us this was not the way to go. But someone very crafty had poked a hole right through its belly.

"Did the Italians build this or the Germans?" my father asked Kazemi.

"Probably the Italians. They were responsible for most of the masterpieces of prewar road construction. They got the design of this road from a plate of spaghetti."

The arch of entrance was tiny. The tunnel was not wide enough for two-way traffic. It was never meant for vacationers. A truck loaded with explosives would have to be very careful not to scrape itself against the sides of the tunnel.

There was an atmosphere of patience and solidarity among the waiting motorists that contrasted with their previous rude fenderings. The driver who almost killed us was out of his car having a cigarette. He was chatting with the motorist behind him who, no doubt, had been passed just as dangerously. We were all waiting to be swallowed by the sacred mountain against which we had allowed a sacrilege. But it was not remorse that bound us together now, it was envy of the skill that defied the earth. The mountains knew that as soon as we learned how, we would start exploding our own holes in their rocky guts.

"Since they built it, no improvements have been made," said my father. "It is exactly as I remember it from the war days."

There was a worker at the mouth of the tunnel standing by a very old telephone. He was speaking with his counterpart on the other side, who was telling him how many cars had entered the tunnel. The system where the last car is given a flag to pass on to the worker at the end of the tunnel would not work. Our national idiosyncrasies forbid many apparently sensible solutions. A few Iranians love to torment minor authorities. Some resent impersonal systems. Others are too important to take orders from a roadworker. Still others become militant over a traffic ticket.

Finally, a line of cars streamed out of the tunnel. A few moments later we were given the green light to pass through. My brother waved at the worker at the old telephone. He waved back.

"Don't distract him, he is counting," I scolded.

We were the last car inside. Suddenly, as though we had been fed to one of Zohaak's snakes, darkness swallowed us. The headlights created sharp passing shadows on the dynamited rocks. There was water seeping through the mountain, and the car in front of us sprayed it on our windshield. Kazemi turned on the wipers.

Instantly the engine died.

"What the . . . !" Kazemi exclaimed in great alarm. "What happened? Is it a fuse?" my father cried in a panic. The headlights were not working. The tunnel grew dark all around us as the taillights of the car ahead vanished to a point. There were only the echoes of dripping water.

"The flashlight in the trunk!" Kazemi shouted and jumped out of the car to get it.

"They will come after us when we fail to show up at the other end," Hojjat assured us.

"Are you sure?" I asked. "The telephone man was not really counting." I was right. At that instant the wailing of horns from tunnel pranksters alerted us that an opposing line of cars had been unleashed against us. Their headlights drew close very fast.

"Signal them or something!" I shouted at my father.

"I can't. No headlights," he said. "Hurry with the flashlight, Kazemi! We only have a few seconds. Pray there are batteries in it."

Kazemi was throwing things around in the trunk, feeling for the flashlight. He could only hear the onrushing cars; for all he knew we could be dead any second.

Finally, just before abandoning the car became inevitable, the thrashing in the trunk stopped and the menacing headlights slowed. I looked back. Kazemi had not wasted any time closing the trunk or coming forward; he was signaling from behind us.

The headlights came slowly closer and pushed us backward out of the tunnel into the welcome daylight.

My father began scolding Kazemi. "Even when you hauled explosives you always jury-rigged everything, never letting a real mechanic touch the truck. I never knew when I pressed the clutch if the horn wasn't going to honk by itself."

Kazemi explained that we had a simple electrical problem that he could fix right away and that there was no need for a "real mechanic." He claimed the engine died because it had overheated and that the fuses blowing had little to do with it. Whatever it was, Kazemi made the car work again and we gave the tunnel another try.

After successfully crossing the tunnel this time, we cozily speculated about the danger we had just avoided. Kazemi, a civil engineer with the ministry of roads, told us that the tunnel is unventilated and even if we had survived the crash, the traffic jam would have put enough carbon monoxide in the air to kill everyone in the tunnel.

The force of gravity was now doing most of the work for the engine. The green meadows of the Caspian region spread below us, alive and fragrant. We were all happy to be alive. My father and Kazemi were reminiscing about the day during the war when they walked into the elegant hotel at Ramsar dragging their muddy boots on the royal carpet.

"The Russians were so happy to see us. We were one of the few trucks that didn't get stopped by the blizzard," Kazemi boasted. "The other drivers thought it was too dangerous to go on. We had to get out in that mess and put on chains. Then the load shifted and we almost went over. No one would have found us till the next summer."

My father picked up from there. "When we reached Ramsar, they were so happy they told us we could go to the hotel for cleanup and rest. We tried to clean off the mud before we went in, but we were so tired we were afraid we would fall asleep on the stone steps."

Ramsar, they explained, was originally named Sakhtsar (hard-headed), but was renamed Ramsar (tame) to please the authoritarian old Shah. The magnificent seaside hotel was built for the old Shah and his guests only, but the recalcitrant monarch had been exiled by the British because he had insisted on his country's neutrality and had not expelled the Germans. After he was forced to abdicate to his son, the resources of Iran were placed at the service of the Allies.

Kazemi and my father were given hot meals and royal rooms, where they took warm baths in the famous mineral waters of Ramsar.

As they finished their story, the Caspian Sea appeared below us and the conversation shifted to wildlife.

"Are there still leopards in those forests?"

* * *

Some years after I came to the U.S., I was surprised to find a news item on the Kandovan Tunnel. Kazemi's theory about a traffic jam had been tragically confirmed. Scores of people had died from carbon monoxide. Despite the enormous wealth showering on Iran, no one, not even Kazemi, had thought to recommend safety improvements in the tunnel. As one friend sarcastically suggested, maybe we were waiting for Western interests to impose it on us.

After the 1979 revolution, Ramsar was predictably given back its old name. I am not sure what has been done about the tunnel. Some matters are harder to predict.

They say people returning from near death remember being in a tunnel. It seems natural. What better poetry for the connection between two places for which there is no in-between? In the past, however, mystics have described the transcendent experience as a crossing of a river. Perhaps technology updates our supposedly universal archetypes. Two decades ago our archetypes were revised by an astounding feat of engineering that took three travelers to a light at the end of the Greatest Darkness and brought them back safely.

The Moon Landing

For a week now we had all been scientists. Words like "gravity," "ascent," "lunar," "perigee," "orbit" flew from our conversations like rockets leaving a busy spaceport. For students across the nation, this summer was different from all others. Previously, scholarly concerns achieved escape velocity for the summer vacation, not to return from their cometlike orbits until fall. This time, however, scientific books and magazines were bought faster than they could be stocked. That summer "hot" was the kinetic energy of air molecules, "sunburn" was the result of solar electromagnetic radiation, and "watermelons" were oblong spheroids.

The Americans were going to the moon, and Iran had one week to catch up.

The Russians had been preparing longer. Their unmanned Luna 15 left a little after Apollo II was launched—it was to be waiting in lunar orbit when the Americans arrived. The Russian motive was not clear. If they wished to further dramatize the American achievement, the crash of Luna 15 succeeded. We ringsiders were disappointed that the race was not closer. On a historic scale, it was a photo finish, but we hoped Luna 15 was secretly manned and that the Americans and the Russians would be elbowing each other for the choicest landing spot. The small step for man should have been a giant leap out the window to be first to tag the moon.

Among the relatives sentiments were mixed and questions were big. "Did God give his permission for this?" "If He becomes angry, will He take it out on everybody or just the Americans?" "What direction do you face when you pray on the moon—flat on your back?" "This victory is the spoils of war—was it not a German rocket that made it possible?"

The censors had taken much of the color out of the on-the-street interviews aired on national television. They were copies of American on-the-street interviews, the main concern being whether or not the money would have been better spent on food. How could we spend all this money to fill our minds when our stomachs were still empty? Stone Age instinct scrutinized the NASA budget and wondered if it was edible. The interviewer avoided asking why Iranians cared how American tax dollars were spent. He might have asked the wrong person and gotten an earful of cousin Iraj's ideas as to where the money really came from and who in the country is responsible for handing over on a platter the nation's resources.

Cousin Iraj was a political beast with a temper. We all worried for him. He was playing Russian roulette with a fully loaded weapon: his mouth. Talking to Iraj was impossible. He listened long enough to calculate one's political whereabouts, then he blasted that position to ruins and offered asylum under the umbrella of his own opinions.

One of Iraj's faithful converts was our manservant, Shafa. Shafa was rooting for the Russians. He imagined the moon to be quite accessible and cursed the West for sabotaging Iran's technological progress. Had they not refused us a steel plant for fear we might overtake them? The Russians, on the other hand, were helping us build our first steel plant. With their help Iran could join the space age. I asked him if he would volunteer if Iran needed an astronaut.

"No," he said flatly.

"Why not, you hypocrite?"

"Wife and children."

"You are so petty."

"You are so young."

Shafa and I had locked horns over the moon landing. This was typical—we were always squabbling over the news. I thought the Americans should win because that way we would see more of the moon. The Russians were unreasonably secretive about their space program. Shafa thought the Russians deserved the lunar prize on moral grounds. He was not an easy opponent. He spent hours with the newspaper, carefully reading between the lines. He did not like TV news. Too visual; no lines that could be read between. He had a theory that whatever Americans do, they do for money.

"Is there money on the moon?" I asked.

"There must be or they wouldn't be going."

"What if they find nothing but rocks?"

"Then they won't go back."

He thought the Russians were racing to the moon to show that idealism prevailed over greed. He was amused that a nation of godless people could wage a holy war against Christians.

Shafa sometimes consulted my father about political issues. He knew it was useless; my father never accepted anyone's invitation to discuss domestic politics. "What I think makes no difference, what I say can get us both into trouble." Iraj used to bait him by suggesting that my father's opinion was probably not tenable anyway. My father's evasion: "I can't make it any more tenable by telling you about it." Shafa once asked him when he thought Iran would have a space program. I knew that my father was very pessimistic about Iran's future. He believed that technology was anathema to our poetic temperament. When the first heart transplant was done, he told me that modernization is like a transplant. To stay alive a little longer, bit by bit we were replacing our parts with dead things.

"Would you rather die than have a transplant?" I asked.

"I don't think I will live long enough to worry about that."

He did not think he would live long enough to see humans land on the moon either. But here he was worrying about how best to evade Shafa's touchy question.

"We are poets and Sufis," he said bitterly. "What can we discover in the universe that the poet Hafiz has not already told us?"

This was not entirely an evasion. Iranians are convinced that Persian poetry cannot be surpassed in depth and beauty. Whereas our claims to monopoly on other forms of art stem from ignorance, I believe that our high opinion of our poetry is justified. Hafiz is the most beloved of the mystic poets. In times of crisis his *Divan* is consulted like an oracle. Street vendors seek out troubled faces in the crowd and sell them scraps of Hafiz's wisdom. Sometimes the oracle is surprisingly explicit and sometimes disappointingly vague. But always the verses flood the crisis with profound spiritual light. If a resolution exists, it will not remain in the shadows.

My father recited a verse that said everything there was to say, and during the mystical silence that always follows the words of Hafiz, Shafa and I did not feel the need for a moon landing.

When domestic politics were not involved, my father was more cooperative. He believed that the scientific yield of the moon program would probably not justify the costs. It was a good way to pass off military research as peaceful science and attain global prestige at the same time. When he explained things so well, I could tell he was lying. The moon landing was an emotional issue for him, and when emotions were involved, he talked like a college professor and acted like an idiot. All through the week of Apollo's journey he made a point of insulting me.

"America has entertained Iranians with its puppet show (he meant the Shah) for this long, and now they have the entire world watching their space show." Such an open criticism of the Shah was quite unlike my father. If I had not known him better, I would have said he was drunk. I asked him if he did not wish there to be a moon landing.

"Do you know what fuels those rockets?" he asked rhetorically. I smelled a trap.

"I think it is liquid hydrogen that combines with. . . ."

"Our oil." He interrupted patronizingly. He was wearing an I-am-so-profound smirk.

120

"What do you mean?" I asked, taking the bait. I had never seen him so candid and wanted him to say more. He shook his head amusedly and said, "That is what happens when you become too American. You stop understanding things even a village boy can figure out."

I walked away chastised. How had I failed him? He had encouraged me all along to admire and emulate Americans. For my own good. Apparently, though, I was not to identify with them to the point of being happy about their successes. I wanted to explain to him that it did not make any difference who landed on the moon. But this was so obvious and deep-felt that if he pretended he did not believe me, I would explode. Getting my goat was his plan, though, even a village boy could see that. He was uncomfortable about the moon landing. I wished he would remarry and take it out on his wife.

Shafa had noticed my father's tauntings and saw his opportunity. Now that my wisdom was being questioned by the master, I was unsure of myself and could be easily defeated in arguments. In this week's frequent debates over the newspaper, he relied less on facts than on insinuations that I was young and gullible. He knew this irritated me and delighted in being able to get back at me for ordering him around.

By the eve of the moon landing, tempers had become quite hot, and it was clear we were going to have popcorn for the show. I lambasted my younger brother for not understanding the significance of the moon landing. The new Iranian imitation-Rolling-Stones record he had bought was monopolizing his sense of awe. Wearing a replica of my father's patronizing smirk, I explained the difference between reality and sci-fi. He told me defiantly that he knew the difference but couldn't see what difference it made. I wanted to torture him until he wept with zealous realization.

To add to the Inquisition atmosphere, cousin Iraj was coming over to spend a few days. I suspected he had been sent away because he had agitated himself to hysteria over the moon landing and his family could not stand him. He might act with more reserve in my father's presence. Iraj had been preaching to fools like me all week, but our glassy, brainwashed stares had resisted his best efforts. What he needed now was a piece of leather on which to gnaw away his frustrations. My hide would come in handy.

Finally the news came over the radio. The Eagle had landed.

For a few moments we stopped being ourselves. My father excit-edly called the relatives to make sure that their radio had said the same thing. They were hard to reach as they were trying frantically to reach us and share the thrill while it was still steaming. I energeti-cally explained to Iraj about "docking" and "rendezvous" and for once he listened. Without being told, Shafa made fresh tea and brought out baklava. Cars were honking outside, and the next door neighbors were louder than ever before.

The radio announcer was the only voice of reason in the din. He reminded us that Iran's newly acquired satellite connection would bring us pictures live from the moon. This was beyond what we could hope for. The Americans had not only landed on the moon but were giving each of us an on-the-spot, private viewing of a very significant moment in the history of life. My father said that if he died right then, it would not matter. What could happen in the future that could surpass this event? Then he wondered whether the rest of humanity did not feel the same way. He predicted gloomily that human history had reached its climax. Iraj agreed and Shafa was an immediate con-vert. I would have joined them, but my brother stopped me.

My younger brother, this thick-skulled, insensitive, arrogant lover of strange music, was unmoved by the giant evolutionary step that had occurred just a few minutes ago under his very nose. So he did not agree that history's greatest hour had just gone by. The shrug of his shoulders was humanity's guarantee against peaking out.

Within hours, however, we wrested our individual minds away from history and became our squabbling selves again. Was the moon landing really that important? The Russians were smart to opt for droids. After all, they achieved the first soft landing on the moon. How did the Americans manage to convince us that man on the moon was so important? I had my hackles back up and Iraj stopped listening to me. Shafa was gloating and my brother was a spoiled brat.

At a time when the Americans were freely giving us their best, we were foolishly holding back a triumph we had achieved long ago: the wisdom of our Sufi poets. That night the world was a confused child in need of comforting. We are a nation of poets trained in the art of wisdom. Where are the mystic verses that explain everything forever? Who will help the lost child cross the street in this rush hour of technology? The descendants of Hafiz were acting like baboons.

The next time Shafa came up with, "Well, we'll see if the Russians get back with the moon rocks first," I told him to shut up. Shafa said nothing, but Iraj told me I had no right to speak to an elder like that, even if he was a servant.

"He is being stupid and so are you."

"Watch it! I am much older than you are."

"Yes, but you are mentally incompetent. That is why they sent you to this loony bin!" I shouted. Iraj turned red. He would have hit me if my father were not there, and I would have hit him back. My father broke into the fight.

"You will not insult a guest in this house. Apologize!" he commanded. But I was in no mood for apologies.

"You too, you imbecile!" I shouted. "Shut up!"

There was silence. This was unprecedented. I had never insulted my father before. He could tell I was ready to escalate further than his dignity could go. There was nothing he could do but grieve. He stood shell-shocked. Shafa and Iraj tried to glare me into shame. Iraj went over to my father and solemnly helped him sit down. I turned around defiantly and left the room.

A few hours later, my brother came to my room and told me that our father had said that if I were willing to apologize to everybody, I could sit with them and watch the moon walk.

"Go tell him that I will apologize to him, but Shafa and Iraj have to apologize to me." He came back and said Shafa agreed, but Iraj would not apologize. I went to the TV room and without saying a word sat straight and stiff in a corner. That was all the apology I would offer. Iraj had his back to where I had chosen to sit and did not adjust his position as politeness dictates. No apology there. Shafa looked up and informed me that the astronauts were about to go out. That was all the apology he would offer.

Like a hippopotamus getting off the bus, the first human on the moon took his time securing his feet on the steps. I felt a door closing quietly behind me: there was no going back. I looked up to see if my father had felt it too. He looked very intense, very sad. If the Russians had been allowed to watch the moon walk, some photographer would have captured the excited defeat on the face of a Russian. But my father had the face of a man who had been left behind, not by a few months or years, but by centuries. And told to shut up to boot.

Then we heard Neil Armstrong say the famous, "One small step for man. . . . " Some magazines, oblivious to the moon dust rhythm of the original, crudely edited this into "One small step for *a* man."

There are those who believe the moon landing never happened. I enjoy believing in outrageous theories, but by dropping that article, Neil made it impossible. If the moon landing were prerecorded on the Earth, some editor would have had him do that line over. There is a rightness to those words that, like the rhythms of the Koran, testify to their own extraordinary origin.

I was humbled that the Americans had the wisdom to let Neil improvise as he stepped on the moon. This answered a very important literary question that a Russian landing may not have provided: What would the first living being to leave the Earth say to his race when he took the first step on another world? Neil did very well considering his difficult landing. Even the best Persian poets drop their articles to color the rhythm. But how I wish it had been Hafiz there in that space suit.

The ancient inscriptions and reliefs, scattered like tattoos over the mountains of Iran, bring to mind the natural question, "How did they get up so high?" The moon landing strongly elicits the same question and that makes it a successful moment. Those forever bootprints on moon powder eternalize all of humanity's greatest accomplishments. My cousin, Bahram, introduced me to the subtleties of monument building. He is a cousin on my mother's side who tutored me for a while. My father normally discouraged much contact with my mother's relatives, but Bahram's mother, Tahereh, insisted. The story is that my mother came to her in a dream, holding up two fingers. Aunt Tahereh took this to mean, "Look after my two children." That is how I became apprenticed to Bahram, the monument builder.

The Monument

On the 2500th anniversary of the monarchy it became necessary to build a monument to the grandeur of Iran. A contest was announced in the newspapers. The best design would be erected. It was a time to be proud. The Shah was telling us that soon Iran would be the fifth most developed nation in the world. His figures were conservative; he could have told us that we were on our way to becoming a superpower and no one would have argued.

Doing as badly in school as I was, I did not feel worthy of citizenship in such a great country. Whoever was propelling this ship to the stars, it was not me. I was dead mass, better blown out the hatch to lighten the load. I confided my feelings of inferiority to cousin Syavosh, who, after a few words of sympathy, said he would ask our cousin Bahram to help me with my studies. Bahram was Syavosh's constant companion and beloved tormentee. They were always together and always debating.

Syavosh had recommended a good tutor. Bahram had done so well in his college entrance examinations that he had gotten his first choice of majors. This was rare. Syavosh, for instance, had tried for biology and been accepted in archeology (he took it anyway to avoid the draft and eventually, like his arranged marriage, became happy with it). Soon after I apprenticed myself to Bahram, my grades improved—but I do not attribute the success to his pedagogical skills. Rather, his passion for tinkering with ideas and his constant debates with Syavosh over any issue whatsoever created a microrenaissance in me that was good therapy for the depression brought about by the contradictions of national delusion.

But Bahram also required some putting up with. His small room at the top floor of his mother's house contained the Smithsonian, Lawrence-Livermore, and the Library of Congress. I always had to make room for myself in the debris. Most of the wreckage could be sat upon, but some artifacts were so holy that the lightest contact with them elicited a scream from their owner. And it was impossible to tell which was which because the various parts of this flotsam were promoted and demoted at the whim of the project at hand.

Bahram was also very impulsive. Early in my apprenticeship, he grew tired of his rooftop room and moved into the greenhouse, Smithsonian and all.

Syavosh ridiculed Bahram at length about the glass house.

"If you wanted to exhibit yourself, you could have a bigger audience from the roof," he mocked. But Bahram dismissed Syavosh's opinion.

"You have no sense of architecture, Syavosh. You could live in a shit pit and say, 'Oh, what a lovely home.'"

Bahram's mother, Aunt Tahereh, was alarmed by the move. She could not reasonably deny her son. Except for sheltering a garden rake left behind by the previous owners of decades ago, the greenhouse served no other purpose. So there was some discussion as to what to do with the rake. When Syavosh offered to give it asylum, Aunt Tahereh had no more excuses and settled for the consolation that if one of Bahram's projects blew up, at least the house was safe.

One day, sitting in the greenhouse, Bahram was giving me a lecture on the battle of Ghadissieh. Syavosh was rummaging through the archives looking for something to read with his tea.

"Where would we be today if the Arabs had not defeated us?" Bahram asked, busily winding a solenoid. When he wound solenoids, he looked like his mother at the sewing machine. "Do you know what those savages did? They burned all our libraries. They said, 'Either it is in the Koran or it is not worth knowing.' We never recovered."

Not having found any literature to suit his mood, Syavosh joined in. "You would think after so many years we would have written some new books," he said, tossing away a magazine.

"We did," Bahram replied, "but the damage had already been done."

"Anyway, there is no evidence that the Arabs burned any books," Syavosh reminded him.

"Have you eaten donkey brains? Where are those pre-Islamic books?"

"Maybe there weren't any."

"A civilization equal to Rome had no books?" Bahram asked incredulously.

"You are still smarting over a battle we lost thirteen centuries ago," Syavosh heckled.

"Of course I am smarting. It burns me to think where we could be now if those barefooted Arabs had not destroyed everything they could not understand."

"They didn't," Syavosh argued. "Civilization flourished under Arab rule. They. . . . "

"That was Persian civilization," Bahram interrupted. "Or what the Arabs left of it."

"So they helped spread our civilization. Why be angry?"

"I am angry because they set us back with their. . . . "

"With their Islam?" It was Syavosh's turn to interrupt. "You'd still be a fire-worshipping Zoroastrian if it were not for the Arabs."

There was a short silence as for the hundredth time Bahram swallowed his nationalism to save his faith. Don't be unfair, Syavosh, I thought. That was a cheap shot.

"Mohammad was different because he had a message from God. Islam is a noble religion," Bahram said dutifully.

"No, Mohammad was a barefoot Bedouin," Syavosh taunted. "And all the fires of Zoroaster did not burn a single book. So much for your 'noble religion.' You are not angry at the Arabs or you would not be such a Moslem. You are angry at history for not pampering Iran. And why should it?"

"And I suppose you are not 'such a Moslem'?" Bahram shot back. "Let me hear you insult the Prophet or even one of the imams. Go on, say something insulting."

"I just called Mohammad a barefoot Bedouin," Syavosh said.

"Which he was proud of. But say something truly insulting. Swear at him, call him names."

Syavosh hesitated. It was Bahram's turn for below-the-belts. "Iran was raped, cousin," Bahram continued. "And our conversion was the rape of our souls. You cannot insult Islam because you, like the rest of us, have fallen in love with the child of this rape."

They had enacted this argument many times before, each time exploring a different subtlety in our relation with Islam. This was always where Syavosh backed down.

"After so many centuries," he chuckled, "we are still prisoners of war."

My schoolwork was affected dramatically by the greenhouse environment. The intimidating mountains of text with no passes now looked shallow and sparse of content: a curriculum to be digested in weeks rather than months. Unfortunately, the Iranian system of education does not allow progress to become immediately apparent. Examinations are held once every three months and these exams alone determine the status of the student. I gained some favor during the term as my response to in-class questions improved, but the argumentative attitude that came with the greenhouse school of thought lost me all my gains: criticism of the teachings is forbidden on the pain of low grades.

My success was marred by yet another circumstance. There had been a rash of cheating in the school that year. Any sudden improvement was suspect. The latest incident involved a student who came from a very influential family. One of the teachers at school had been retained as tutor for this boy. The teacher leaked some of the final exam questions to his pupil in order to make up for the failure of the tutorials. He had underestimated the boy's capacity for bold enterprise: the questions went on the market. I too was offered them at a price I could afford, but, thanks to Bahram, I saved my money.

When I went to get my report card, the principal, certain that I was among the renegade student's clients, tossed it to me across the desk in disgust. He had decided there was nothing he could do about the cheating except be more careful next time. If he punished anyone, he would have to punish the boy who sold the questions. That was a battle he was wise enough to avoid. I wanted to tell him that I had a tutor, but I knew the word *tutor* meant something else to him these days. He was letting me keep my good grades, what else could I ask for?

I went straight to Bahram's house to show him my report card and to tell him gleefully that I had done so well the principal thought I had cheated. I knew he would ask me if I would have bought the questions had I needed them, and on the way, I was thinking of an answer. This was Bahram's influence: he had taught me how to pose my own questions.

When I reached Bahram's residence, he was still at the university. Aunt Tahereh asked me to go inside the house, but I preferred to stay in the greenhouse and look around. There were sketches of buildings, architecture magazines, and Persian history books on top of the older litter. My aunt brought me some cherry *sharbat* (a sweet drink) with ice to drink and asked if I could guess what her son was working on. I guessed he was working on a mausoleum of sorts.

"What mausoleum? He is working on the Shah's monument," she said, offended.

"Oh, the competition!" I realized my faux pas. "Well, the Taj Mahal is a mausoleum," I added quickly.

"Your mother was like you," she smiled, "always trying to fix what she wrecked."

When Bahram walked in, Syavosh was with him.

"It looks too much like a mausoleum," Syavosh was complaining.

"What do you expect it to look like, a bathhouse? A mausoleum is meant to commemorate and so is a monument," Bahram explained.

"You must avoid that pitfall. Only then will your work be original," Syavosh warned.

"How?" Bahram wanted to know.

"For one thing, don't emphasize the vertical axis—otherwise people are going to think someone is buried at the foot of it."

"You are thinking about this too mechanically. The most important consideration should be whether or not our evolution is reflected perceptively," Bahram said.

"You mean like those from-ape-to-man pictures?"

"Only backwards," Bahram laughed. "From great empire to third-world nation."

"The tomb of Iran," Syavosh concluded.

"No." Bahram became serious. "We will survive. That is our greatness. This monument is not going to lie. It will not glorify us. It is a reminder of our stubbornness."

I picked up the drawings and looked at the structure again. It was solid and willing to wait. It did not pretend to move. One could easily throw a blanket in its shade and take a nap. What I had mistaken for immortality and life after death was really just plain perseverance.

Syavosh was ponderously shuffling the drawings.

"They are not going to like it, Bahram. They want glory."

"Then they will have to import it. I am not going to lie."

"It is not a lie, it is *taghieh*." Syavosh said. Taghieh is the Shiite doctrine that allows deception in times of adversity. By appearing to deny their faith, the early Shiites avoided execution. Syavosh was using the term in a very modern sense, however; the taghieh doctrine originally did not encourage *self*-deception and, as Bahram pointed out, was to be used sparingly under conditions when the faith was in peril.

"We *are* in peril," Syavosh protested. "The survival ability that you are so proud of comes from our willingness to do with reality as we please."

"It is shameful," Bahram said.

"No. We would have perished if after every domination by the Arabs, the Mongols, the Turks, we had felt defeated. But we didn't; we weathered the defeats. Today we are dominated by the West. So why not believe we are the fifth most industrialized nation in the world until this progress thing blows over and we can go back to drinking our tea in peace?"

"When will that be?" Bahram asked.

"Not long—a few hundred, maybe a thousand years."

"They will be in the stars by then," Bahram sighed.

"Our own star is the most comfortable to live under," Syavosh said reassuringly.

Bahram worked for a few more weeks on his monument. Aunt Tahereh was concerned that the project was not healthy for him. He went out for walks at night and did not return until the early morning hours. He wished to put more glory into his design but did not want it to be phony. It was hard digging. He had searched the rubble of recent history for evidence of accomplishment but found only impressions of laurels fossilized on the nation's buttocks.

One night a cat followed him home. She stayed for a week and then ran away. Bahram did not know much about cats and gave it nothing but milk. He named her Iran because the map of Iran looks like a cat. He said he believed the cat should be our national symbol just like the bear and the eagle represented Russia and America.

". . . because cats have many lives."

I don't know what happened to his entry or whether he managed to put in enough glory to make it competitive. All I know is that it did not win.

The design that did win was completed shortly after I came to America. Bahram sent me a postcard with a picture of it. I am not sure if he *chose* that particular card or whether it happened to be handy. He did not mention anything about the picture.

Even though the monument is a concrete structure that mixes Achaemenian, Islamic, and modern motifs, it reminds me of an Eiffel Tower truncated at the waist. A mausoleum to the 2500 years of monarchy that ended soon thereafter, the monument stands today proud and accomplished like a good grade on a report card. Whether it was earned or bought, I am still deciding.

Bahram left Iran after the revolution. I have not been in touch, but I hear from his younger brother that he is in Germany. Bahram has a good business in that country, though he jokes that in all the time he has been there he has yet to be invited to a German house for dinner. I do not know if he is blaming his own adaptive skills or accusing a hundred million Germans of a uniform lack of hospitality. I certainly miss hearing him doubt and debate himself.

While we were both in Iran, I accidentally joined the international community in Tehran. I met many foreigners, and though I did not get invited to dinner either, the experience whetted my appetite for the cross-cultural life.

Of Bears and Chromosomes

One year the rivalry among the relatives as to who is the best parent intensified to such heights that my father played his big trump and enrolled me in a school run by Americans.

Since I had passed the prerequisite English test with colors at half-mast, the school was concerned that I might not be able to survive the all-English curriculum. But my father's enthusiasm caused them to abandon their good sense. They enrolled me.

The old school building slept in the shade of wise evergreens. There were cool ponds, quiet arches, and brooding niches. In the old days this had been a hospital. Later it became a missionary school and gradually evolved into a secular center of learning.

On the blue tiles above the entrance was written in English and Farsi, "You shall know the truth and the truth shall make you free."

The Persian translation was done very literally and looked awkward. A better translation would have left more tile space for the calligrapher to show more graphically how freedom follows truth. As it stood, I pictured a large American named "Mr. Truth," who carried a hefty jangle of keys on his belt. He stood arms akimbo in front of a row of locked doors and occasionally let someone out.

But English translates better into Farsi than vice versa. The English teacher was overwhelmed by my ability to write things she could not understand. My essays often came back with a red "What are you trying to say?!" or "What is your opening paragraph doing at the end of the essay?!" During numerous and compassionate conferences with me, she explained that no one has any business writing anything until he has mastered the essay. The essay, she said, needs to let the reader know what it is about and quickly. The first sentence of the first paragraph has to have a very good reason for doing anything else.

Such impatience, I thought.

Iranians do not read often and when they do, it is like a stroll through the garden. Reading a book could be a month's project. For Americans, reading is a daily physiological need and it is understandable that without the you-are-here organization of their writing styles, their minds would quickly clutter. Once when I did not turn in my English homework, I heard through the grapevine that the English teacher had expressed some happiness.

I may have been a particularly hard case, however. The other foreign students included Turks, Greeks, English, Israelis, Japanese, Lebanese. They had some difficulty keeping up with the Americans, but acclimated quickly. These students were the sons and daughters of foreigners working in Iran. The Iranians in the school were, with few exceptions, from wealthy backgrounds. They came to school every morning with the latest silver spoons in their mouths.

The culture shock was stunning. Day after day I went home with more on my mind than I could process. Coeducation, upper-class snottiness, bake sales, Spiderman lunch boxes, Bibles, Shakespeare, Greeks. Commuting between cultures was more difficult than being stranded in one. I felt thoroughly out of my environment, like an oyster-shell ashtray. I could not wait until Mr. Truth let me out.

Relief came from behind the Iron Curtain. One day a Polish boy named Zygmundt appeared in our midst. How our friendship developed is mostly a mystery. He did not have any of the problems that I was having. He was fluent in English and did not write his essays inside out. He had traveled across the world and was at ease in the melting pot. The Iranian aristocracy kept its distance, as a sweep of his chain-saw wit could reduce the loftiest of them into kindling. Real challenges were so rare in his life that I wondered how he kept from being bored.

We had some difficulty communicating at first. He seemed uninterested in Persian, and it had not occurred to me that Polish could be a language. English did not work because, as presented to me by the English teacher, it was too sensible to allow much content. So we decided on French as the language of our friendship. We were both taking French at the time, and we felt that we had served our sentence of hard labor conjugating verbs and were ready to slide freely on those sensuous surfaces of sound.

This did not please the French teacher. What we spoke was a monstrous mutation of what we had been taught. Sometimes if the desired French word was in hiding, we raided the nearby English synonyms and tortured *them*. Bad grammar was no object in getting the point across, and we had vowed never to let the dictionary interrupt the flow of our conversation. Zygmundt suggested we should leave letters so that in case we were murdered, the French teacher would be implicated.

But what Zygmundt and I had in common was what we were not allowed to talk about. The only time I remember him showing any awareness of the situation of our respective countries was when he found out that the American community in Iran referred to the Shah as "Ralph." He laughed until he was exhausted.

To some extent the nickname was American irreverence, but to a large degree it made sense. If an Iranian overheard them say, "Ralph is stateside groveling for arms," he would not be contaminated.

Our avoidance of political issues was one reason for our apparent lack of interest in each other's heritage. Once you start talking about your parents and your childhood and what you call a sycamore tree, you are on your way to discussing politics. I think that is one reason people talk about the weather when they don't want to talk: your souls keep flying out to the sky instead of staying between your faces. All I knew about his background was that his parents were Polish embassy employees.

He knew nothing about my family, but my father was sure that he did. "They keep close tabs on their people, especially if they are in a Western-influence country," he said. "They probably know who all his friends are."

My father did not approve of our friendship. "I spend all this money to send you to an American school and you come back with a Polish friend?"

"But Father, he is the best student in the class. He is brilliant."

"There are no brilliant Americans?"

"Yes, but for one thing they are mostly married."

"Married? At their age?"

"They have girlfriends or boyfriends very early on and that is where their loyalties go. They have good friendships, but love always comes first."

"So why don't *you* get a girlfriend?"

I was too shy to talk openly about my favorite girl with my father, so I changed the subject. "Besides, they do strange things I do not understand."

"Like what?"

"They have student government," I laughed.

"That is *good*. Why don't you participate in that? They are training their children in democracy."

"The student government has no power. It holds dances and bake sales, but all real decisions are made by faculty. What sort of democracy are they training them for, anyway?"

This irritated him. "You are there to learn what is good about them, but all you do is notice their faults," he scolded. "Student government teaches organizing skills, and you have a lot to learn from them. Even if you want to grow up to be a revolutionary, you can use what you learn as a bake-sale politician. I want you to start getting involved."

"I would be very humiliated if you made me do such a thing," I said, drawing a line.

"Why?"

"I don't know. I would have to pretend I cared about things I don't care about."

He softened and pointed out that if it were not for school government, I would not have learned this lesson about real-world politics. His money was not being wasted after all. Then he decided he would confide in me.

"The personality type that goes after power is not suited for leadership in the modern world. They would do all right with a tribe of baboons but . . . . " He had a habit of stopping in midsentence so that I could finish it for him. That way he knew if I was paying attention.

"But bake sales are far too important to be entrusted to baboons," I finished.

"Bake sa . . . ?" He got the joke midsentence. "When I was in America, I noticed their democracy is not what they advertise it to be. They seem to think the vote is magic. But voters let themselves be manipulated, and they do not have much power. They are satisfied to equate the casting of ballots with democracy. It really is the same all over the world," he said bitterly. "It is as though the form of government is determined by how best a people can be manipulated."

I took advantage of this brief flash of sincerity and pushed ahead with my grievance against my American classmates.

"So who has told them to act like they own this country?"

"They do own the country," he said matter-of-factly.

"Then why don't they stick another star on their flag, call it the state of Iran, and stop banning books?"

The non sequitur about the books clued him in. As long as I was airing my own concerns he had listened, but once I plunged into unoriginal rhetoric he hardened again.

"You have been listening to Iraj again, haven't you?" My cousin Iraj was, among other things, rashly political. He was very curious about my American school and was always probing. When he found out the school had a good library, he asked me to check out some books for him.

"Get me Lenin's book on imperialism," he ordered. When I brought him the book, he foamed at the mouth and hit the roof.

"Why is it that their people read whatever they want and we get thrown in jail for it? Right under our very noses, in our very country, they allow their children to read books *our* children can't." He threw the book back at me to return it; he had already read it through the underground press.

Since Poland suffered the same repression as Iran, I could not understand what Zygmundt was doing in an American school. I could not ask him without bringing up things we were not allowed to bring up. But this was no obstacle for our friendship, and we spent more and more time together talking "French."

Our favorite topic was girls. Neither of us had a girlfriend because the girls we were interested in were Iranian and their families did not believe in boyfriends. I had given up, but Zygmundt was persisting.

"Zygmundt, if she accepts you, would you still spend time with me?"

His eyes brightened. "If she accepts me, we will have so much more to talk about."

When we were not talking about "her," we played chess. Between moves, he did pencil drawings. Once he drew a picture of the surface of the moon. He had weathered the edges of the craters so that they were not so jagged, as though the moon had acquired a thin atmosphere. The effect was stunning. I asked to borrow it so that I could show my father how talented my friend was. The move backfired. My father said he did not want me to get in the habit of lending and borrowing with a Polish national.

"Why do you insist on worrying me? I want you to remember you are not in America. I know, it is my fault that you are not raised to realities and can't think for yourself, but you have to trust my judgment here."

The next time Zygmundt wanted to lend me something I was reluctant. It was a biology paper he had written.

"It is brilliant if I say so myself," he bragged. "You must tell me what you think."

"Zygmundt, I am not good at these things. The teacher hates me. Remember, I am the only one in class who could not grow bacteria."

"That is because you boiled the flask, you idiot."

138

"I know, you told me before."

"What were you trying to do, grow indestructible bacteria?"

"I report only to the Fuehrer."

"That is not funny. Here, read this," he said, shoving the papers in my face.

"This is virtually a book. I will get bored. Almost all the faculty has read it and they think it is wonderful. Isn't that enough?"

"No, I want *you* to think it is wonderful. You have trouble telling me how brilliant I am, so if you say it is good, then I *know* that it is."

"All right, I admit it. You are a genius. Now spare me the reading."

"It explains why bears cannot successfully mate with humans," he said, enticingly dangling the papers in front of my eyes.

"Let me see that."

I borrowed an oversized book from the library and stuck Zygmundt's paper in it. Then I spent the weekend behind the big book.

It was a treatise on cytotaxonomy. It discussed critically the comparative studies of chromosomes in classifying species. Although completely beyond the range of our curriculum, the topic was explained and illustrated with ingenious clarity. The boy should be writing textbooks, I thought. It was frustrating not to be able to show this to my father. The best part of my life was hiding behind a big book on race cars.

The next school day I returned the paper to him.

"What did you think? Was it not brilliant?" he asked.

"It was good," I said noncommittally.

"I can tell you think it is brilliant. Do not pretend."

"It is not that," I said.

"Then what is it?" He was very concerned.

"Well, I was a little disappointed."

"What? You must not have read it."

"I read it and I think it has a serious flaw."

"How can you improve it?" He was almost weeping.

"It has too many chromosomes and not enough bears."

He chased me around the school throwing pebbles and yelling things in a language I had not heard before. When we were both holding our bellies, gulping for breath, I told him his paper should be in the biology book. He lit up but immediately saddened.

"You will write?"

"Write what?"

"Letters. I am going back to Poland soon."

* * *

Our last conversation was about keeping in touch. We had just exchanged addresses.

"Write every week if you want," he said.

"OK. . . . Zygmundt?"

"What?"

"Nothing."

"You do not want me to write, do you?"

"Just be careful what you say. The censor reads them you know."

"I had no idea," he said sarcastically. "All right, I'll try to keep Ralph out of it. You too, don't say anything stupid. Just stick to bears and chromosomes. Maybe we can even play chess by mail."

A month later my father threw a letter on my desk. It was open. I looked at him accusingly.

"It came that way. If I had opened it, I would have sealed it back up," he said.

"What does it say anyway?" I said gruffly.

"I did not read it. It would be pointless after the censor had seen it."

The letter was innocuous, almost vapid. How was I? A few people to say hello to. Humid this time of year. (He was allowing me to set the depth of our communication.) At the end of the letter he had written a code that had probably raised the censor's eyebrow. It said P-Qkt 4 (pawn to queen's knight four): the very irregular Polish chess opening. Though I wanted to I never wrote back.

In the years that followed, both Poland and Iran rattled their cages and so shook the world. I wonder what side he has taken. He probably wonders the same thing about me.

Well, Zygmundt, the "French" have a saying, "Better late than never." P-K4.

The spring after Zygmundt left, Aunt Monavar died. Though I was close to her, I could not bring myself to go to her funeral. One feels obligated to grieve at funerals and grief is difficult to turn off and on at will. Like labor pains it swells and subsides. Monavar's long illness gave her enough time to make her peace with death. Also, in the way that matters most to a mother, her life was fulfilled: she raised her child well. But in other respects she left many loose ends. My younger daughter reminds me of Monavar, and I must make sure that as she weaves her young life, the strands of her great-aunt's unfinished wisdom are passed to her.

The Husband

The last few weeks I had stopped taking the bus. It was only an hour's walk from school to the hospital, and I needed time to trample the sidewalk, away from the distractions of the crowded city bus.

First there was the man who had seizures between the most crowded stops. His assistants, disguised as ordinary passengers, gave him medicine money and urged others to make up the difference. Then came the man with the bamboo flute. He played so well I felt bad that such talent had to beg for survival. Most recently a little boy had been singing classical poetry in a bleating voice. Hands shuffled in pockets as the listeners panicked to ransom the honored verses.

The bus, so packed with life and struggle, was bad preparation for the hospital visit. An hour's lonely walk and I would not reek of life when I appeared at Aunt Monavar's deathbed.

The Husband

She was on the highest floor, her bed facing a panoramic view of the Alborz Range. When I said hello, the living half of her tried to smile. She seemed happier than I had ever seen her. Whatever had damaged her brain must have also destroyed the bitterness.

We would sit staring at the mountains for a long time, then she would tap me lightly on the back: go home and eat your dinner. Soon her son, Iraj, would be coming back from work to keep her company. Her husband, Madani, was discouraged from making visits. The relatives did not like him and blamed him for Monavar's illness. Madani was not one to insist on his rights at all costs. He mostly stayed out of the room to avoid ugly scenes in front of his dying wife.

When Monavar first fell ill many years before, I wondered why Madani was blamed. I asked here and there, but clearly, a family secret was involved. The causes I was given—he yells a lot, he is stingy, he is ill-mannered—did not explain a defective heart valve. Once I asked Monavar why, if she were so unhappy, had she married him. She was in the kitchen boiling sour cherries for jam. She said she married very young. When their father died, the oldest brother was only thirteen. He did all he could to provide for them, but the girls had to be married off quickly to ease the burden. She first met Madani when he rented a room at their house. He was from the rural Luristan region and had come to the city to take a civil service job. When he was away at work, young Monavar used to sneak into his room to play with his stationery.

"He had a fancy brass inkwell. It was shaped like a tower and held three colors of ink: red, green, and blue. There were boxes of colored pencils and neatly bound notebooks. I made cities out of the stationery. The tower was always downtown, and the erasers were boats that floated over the waves of colored pencils. When they told me he had asked for me, I consented right away. I was really marrying the stationery."

"Did he let you play with them after you got married?" I asked.

"After a woman marries, she loses her childhood quickly. People treat her differently even if she is in fact still only a child."

"Why is it that the relatives do not like Madani?" I asked bluntly.

"He is such a boor, does not understand civilization. He should have stayed with his own people in their village. He is an embarrass-

143

ment when we go out. I always have to remind him to keep his voice down. He yells as though he is still herding sheep. You will not find anyone stupider than a Lur."

"Why do people from the village yell when they talk?"

"I don't know. Maybe it is because they do not wash their ears often."

The jam making was a rare event. She was not allowed to work because of her condition.

"I am going crazy being cooped up in the house when I am not even allowed to do housework. What am I supposed to do? Will you ask your father to get me a job in his office?" she begged, giving me a taste of the hot jam.

"I have asked him many times. He gets angry at me for not minding my own business. He says you are too sick to work."

"I will die of boredom first. Did you tell him that?"

"Yes, I told him everything you told me to tell him."

"What did he say?"

"Nothing. He thinks you are crazy. He does not believe women should work in offices."

"Then why did he find Tooran a job?" she demanded enviously.

"Tooran's husband is very ill. They need the extra income. My father says you want to work just so you can feel important. That is not a good enough reason to risk your life."

Tooran, ever the agitator, had been using her job to torment her younger sister, Monavar. At every opportunity she told Monavar in tantalizing detail of the glamorous life of the office—conferences, memos, power plays, promotions, intrigue, gossip.

"I am getting a driver's license. Maybe at my next pay raise I will buy a car." "I have enrolled in classes to finish my diploma. I wonder what I will study in college that will further my career."

Monavar, who received only rebuke for any work she did, chewed on her own insides at Tooran's successes. My father had warned Tooran that if she did not stop her silliness, he would arrange for her dismissal. But she called his bluff; she knew he would not deprive the children of a source of income for something their mother had done. Tooran knew everyone's weaknesses and never did anything she could not get away with.

144

Once Monavar went out on her own and secretly started working at a tailor's in the neighborhood. She was immediately discovered and brought home. Iraj told her that such work was beneath her and that he would pay her whatever she expected to earn if she would promise not to do this again. Monavar promised nothing.

"What do you expect me to do then?" she cried.

"Watch television, read magazines, take naps," Iraj ordered.

"Is that going to cure me? Is that why I should start living in a crypt already?"

The question of a cure came up often. The doctor, a Western-educated heart specialist, acting with proper Western medical ethics, had laid out the choices without making up their minds for them. Surgery, drugs, or nothing. Surgery might or might not help and there was a risk she could die on the operating table. Drugs would help the heart but would increase the risk of stroke. There was also the possibility that, left to herself, she might live as long as she would otherwise.

Monavar did not make the choice easier. She never talked to Madani about anything serious, preferring to let the very young Iraj make the decisions. But when Iraj tried to discuss the choices with her, she said with resignation, "Whatever you tell me to do I will do."

She was worried that Iraj would be too extravagant and that an operation would wipe out their savings without curing her. And what if she was cured? What then? She would live five, maybe ten more years, during which she would sap the resources of her only son even further. Not knowing what to do, Iraj postponed the decision by putting Monavar on drugs.

The relatives made harsh judgments against Iraj and his father for not opting for surgery. They believed that the two of them had conspired to save their money, leaving Monavar to die. One could never be sure if such opinions had any basis. Would Monavar not have said something if she were being wronged? No. Even if her son were acting against her best interests, she would sacrifice her life so that he would not be inconvenienced.

There is a story of a cruel seductress who asks a man for his mother's heart. The son ruthlessly tears out the heart, but in his eagerness to rush the prize to his lover, he stumbles and hurts himself.

As he is brushing the dust away from his clothes, the heart comes to life to worry over her son's skinned knee.

Monavar patterned her motherhood on this model. This made it difficult for young Iraj to fathom her best interests. Should he let her die because she would be happier if *his* financial interests were served? Or should he drag her to the operating table, never knowing if she was resisting for his sake or hers?

Monavar's love for Iraj had always been a mixed blessing. When, with his first paycheck, he bought a long-awaited tape recorder, Monavar made a beautiful cloth cover to keep the dust away. But despite such care, within a few weeks the tape recorder stopped working. The repairman found a half-rial piece short-circuiting the wires. Monavar had dropped it in to protect the machine from evil spirits. The hardest part for Iraj was asking her to stop putting money in the machine without revealing to her that she was responsible for the damage. It would have crushed her to know she had done something to hurt her precious child.

Iraj's love for his mother was equally puzzling. He, with help from the relatives, had buried his mother alive to prolong her life. Fortunately, Monavar never tired of seeking ways to escape to the realm of the living.

One day she called me on the phone and said she had read a story in a magazine and wished me to hear it. This was odd, why did she not wait and give me the magazine to read when I was there?

The story was about a Lur working in the city who was recruited by the central government to help quell a Lur uprising. She was quite a storyteller. I was completely enthralled and urged her to go on when she stopped. She said the story was a serial and that she would read me the sequel next week. I waited a week and went to her house to ask for the rest of the story. She pulled out a handwritten manuscript from under her carpet. I suspected as much. The hero in the story was unmistakably Madani. She made me promise not to tell anyone about it or she would stop writing.

Week after week she read me what she had completed. After some initial successes, Madani is captured by the Lurs, who want to put him to death; instead, he challenges them to let him endure their traditional tests of manhood. He passes their tests and wins their admiration. Then suddenly, in a dramatic revelation of his origin, he gives a moving speech for national unity in his mother tongue. They would surrender to him, but ironically he has found his roots and it is *he* who becomes a convert and takes up the cause. His wife and only son are taken hostage by the secret police. They will be released if Madani, who is now a brilliant leader of the uprising, surrenders. Plans are being made for a rescue, but there is treason afoot.

She was still writing when she had the stroke. Several times at the hospital I asked her what happened to the manuscript. She smiled helplessly with half her face. I went home and, on a large piece of cardboard, drew the alphabet. She could not write, but maybe she could point out the letters. When I brought the alphabet to the hospital, Madani, who usually waited in the halls, told me she was being massaged by a German doctor. I went inside. The young doctor was in the process of turning her over and acted surprised. He asked me irritably if the patient was my mother. I said she was my aunt. The doctor ordered me to leave, as only immediate family could be present during a massage.

"She *is* immediate family. She is my aunt," I told him, but he sternly pointed to the door. Monavar was limp in his arms like a scene from *Gone with the Wind*. She had that half-smile on her face.

The next day she died.

I found out when I walked into the hospital with my alphabet board and saw the relatives weeping in the lobby. Tooran was leading Iraj away from Madani, who was grabbing onto his son.

"Get away from him, you murderer," she whispered venomously. Madani said nothing but clung to his son, who, overcome by grief, was helpless to speak for himself. I turned around before anyone saw me and did my mourning on the long walk back home.

Much later, I asked Iraj if he had found any manuscripts in his mother's belongings. He said Monavar wrote a lot—which manuscript did I mean? I explained. He said he had not seen it. Also, he told me my alphabet board would have been useless in her condition.

Madani remarried quickly after Monavar's death. This made the relatives hate him even more. I searched my memory for clues as to where this hostility began, and recalled a conversation from when I was much younger.

Farabi, Tooran's husband, had been drinking to celebrate the marriage of a nephew. In the roar of the festivities, he bragged about how in the old days in the army they used to go whoring on Thursday nights and how the army doctor treated everyone for gonorrhea whether they showed symptoms or not. Cousin Daryoosh was embarrassed by his father's confessions and wished to clear his name.

"But you never really had gonorrhea, did you?" he asked eagerly. Farabi sobered slightly but not enough. "Son, in those days you were not considered a man until you got some sort of venereal disease."

"Yes, you tried, but you never really got anything, right?"

"Well, the friends and I *did* go out a lot on Thursday nights."

"But you did not become sick," Daryoosh insisted.

"I wouldn't call it a sickness. It is so easy to cure, you know."

Daryoosh pursued this no further. He had not succeeded in talking his father out of the truth. Later, when he and I were alone, he tried to make excuses for his father. With a tone much like his mother he said, "Monavar's husband has done a lot worse. At least *my* father was honest about it. Madani didn't even tell his wife."

"Monavar got a disease from Madani?" I asked.

"Much worse. Why do you think they have only one child? You think they stopped?"

"Does he still fool around?"

"How should I know? But it is not whether a man whores or not, it is whether he is honest about it with his wife so she can see a doctor in time."

Daryoosh may have been making up the story or he may have heard it from someone who made it up. Iranians sometimes invent stories about people they are angry at. They assume for every lie they make up about their adversary, there is an equally incriminating truth that they happen not to know. Why let the guilty escape justice when evidence can be so easily dreamt up? As soon as the relationship is patched, however, the cleanup begins and the stories are denied by the manufacturer. But if one is not passing judgment on Madani's character, there is no reason to doubt that such a tragedy could have befallen his family. As Farabi said, you are not considered a man until. . . .

The Husband

. . .

Once I missed my bus stop. A comedian was performing on the bus, and he was too engaging to walk out on. I ended up in a strange part of town, probably familiar to Farabi and Madani. I called my father to tell him not to worry if I was late.

"Where are you now?" he inquired. I gave him the cross streets.

"What the hell are you doing *there*!" he shouted. "Stay right where you are. I will send someone after you."

"I am fine. I am just waiting for the next bus to arrive."

"How much money do you have on you?" he asked urgently. I said it was not enough to take a taxi.

"Thank God," he breathed. "Get home as soon as you can."

Whoever thought up the original hare and tortoise story was an old soul. The parable, such a wonderful caveat against overconfidence, is also an allegory for the triumph of Time over Youth. I censor the latter interpretation when children are listening, though they would not understand anyway that God has rigged the race so that, wise or foolish, lazy or eager, the rabbit will never win. Let the children believe, as long as they can, that Time was created when they first opened their eyes and that their world is as everlasting as a lullaby in mother's arms.

Our clan was losing its older members one by one. After Monavar died, the tortoise crept up on Farabi.

The Mullah with No Legs

The mullah with legs always came in a shiny taxi. Framed by the richly tasselled, tinted windows of the bright orange car, he arrived in a rumbling rainbow of flashing chrome. The apparition briefly scintillated in front of the house next door while the mullah got out and Aunt Tooran's neighbor, the carpenter, rushed out to pay the driver. Soon the powerful P.A. system, courtesy of the carpenter, would blast the neighborhood with the mullah's mournful Arabic.

The mullah with no legs always came mounted on the back of a man wearing faded plaid. The two appeared on Aunt Tooran's doorstep, a large hump of brown on top of a pale tangle of rectangles. A subtle movement of the mullah's elbow directed his mount to clop up the stairs into the hall. There the plaid young man would remove his shoes and bring the mullah into the guest room. A few more elbow signals and the mullah would be propped up ready to perform. The young man would leave the room and sit on the mosaic steps of the hall entrance.

I always volunteered to take the mount his dish of *halvah* and glass of tea. (Halvah is a caramel-colored confection of flour, sugar, rosewater and saffron with the texture of modeling clay.) While the mullah talked, the mount and I played the Iranian game of learn everything, reveal nothing. He was curious about who was who in our family; I mainly wished to know how the mullah lost his legs. Tooran had told me that she thought the mullah was born without his legs.

The mount's curiosity was not idle: one needs to know who can pull what strings. My curiosity was teenage fascination with dismemberment. I was no match for him, which is just as well. He used the knowledge he captured from me to make things easier for himself and his clan. I longed to be able to tell the neighbor's children that while their mullah was sleek, our mullah had lost his legs to a crocodile while he was studying at the seminary in Egypt.

I envied the neighbors for their mullah. Our mullah did not wear a bright green shawl; he, unlike the neighbor's mullah, did not consider himself to be a direct descendant of the Prophet. He did not come and go in flashy taxis. I had seen him in the streets, always riding the plaid, never on anything with wheels. He did not have the neighbor mullah's elegance and youth. He wore such an old *abba* (mantle) that passersby, thinking he was a crippled beggar, stopped to give him money. He gratefully accepted and sent loud prayers after the alms-giver. Unlike the neighbor's mullah, he did not glitter like a freshly opened present, but he was a decent man with close ties to God. The first real beggar that crossed his path would receive the misdirected alms with instructions to pray after the kindly passerby who had made the mistake.

Looking back, I am not so envious, as it seems each mullah filled a particular need. The carpenter was a businessman. It was important to his livelihood that the neighbors be aware that he was a devout Moslem. Being fully regulated by the agencies of heaven, devout businessmen do not overcharge or misrepresent their product. So he had set aside an advertising budget that paid for a flashy mullah and a P.A. system that spared no one within miles. With God's help, his business was doing well enough that he was even thinking of investing in the new and risky business of raising American chickens.

Aunt Tooran needed a different kind of intercession. Her husband, Farabi, was very ill. The logo mullah would have been useless to her. She needed a mullah who could bring cures, console the grieving, and give the strength of faith to the dying. Also, it is believed that God lends a kinder ear to the handicapped, so a mullah with no legs appeared heaven-sent.

Because the mullahs addressed different markets, their visits need not have caused a rivalry, but Aunt Tooran and the neighbor's wife, neither of whom could withstand much tranquility, had fashioned a conflict out of this seemingly unpromising material. Their previous battle had been mercilessly resolved by the fruit and vegetableseller who had started to stagger the opening of new crates of grapes throughout the morning. This way, early risers like Tooran did not ravage the best grapes, leaving only mushed ones to sleepers-in like the carpenter's wife.

The rivalry had started when, one day at the marketplace, Tooran informed the fruit and vegetableseller that she was accompanying her husband to a pilgrimage to Mashad. The shrine of Imam Reza in Mashad is the source of many miraculous healings. Men who visit the shrine come back bearing the once-prestigious title of *Mashadi*. Tooran also let it be known that in these godforsaken days not enough pilgrimages were being made, the pilgrimage funds being wasted on P.A. systems.

The news and commentary were intended for the ears of the carpenter's wife, who told the fruit and vegetableseller that her husband was saving for a trip to Mecca. This, the most prestigious pilgrimage of all, would earn him the title *Haji*. Many businessmen in the bazaar bear this title; it is so important to business that some people use the title even before making the pilgrimage. If his business is obviously doing well and if a man is obviously rich, it is a disgrace for him not to have made the pilgrimage, which is required of all who can afford it.

The carpenter's wife also added, for the enlightenment of the fruit and vegetableseller, that chadors with little flower designs were undignified as they defeated the very purpose of the chador, which is to keep visual attention away from the wearer. Tooran was a handsome woman with no incentive for deflecting attention away from herself. Except on solemn occasions, her chadors were extremely short and botanical.

From then on, a rivalry ensued as to who was more Moslem than whom. I doubt that the mullahs ever became fully aware that they were being used as pawns in a contest of piety, but the broadcasting mullah may have suspected something from the number of times he was requested to mention the undesirability of flower patterns on chadors. Because of the spiritual depth of our mullah, morale was better on our side, but the neighbor clearly had the upper hand in hardware. As the neighborhood was entirely Moslem to begin with, the P.A. system would not make any converts, but it was overwhelming in its ability to convert electricity to loud Arabic. Many nights we lay awake to the lullaby of amplified Koran, dreaming of ways to reconcile Tooran and the carpenter's wife.

A good way for neighbors to forgive each other is provided by the *nazr* custom. Plates of food and pieces of sacrificial lamb are distributed among the neighbors so that they might add their prayers to those of the benefactor. One can hardly continue to bear a grudge against a person who sends a plate of food, requesting in return a prayer for the recovery of a loved one. When the foe brings back the empty plate and the plate owner says, "You did not have to return it so clean, I would have washed it myself," good will is rekindled. The neighbor made frequent nazrs because only the youngest of her seven children could get passing grades without divine intervention. Aunt Tooran also made nazrs because of her ailing husband, but now the plate of *nazri* appeared to be hypocritical piety and intensified the rivalry even further. With the olive branch interpreted as yet another weapon, the neighbor's children continued to fail and Aunt Tooran's husband continued to die.

Farabi's illness had started soon after the evening known to Tooran as "The Night the Owl Came." It was a few months before the mullah with no legs entered our lives. Aunt Tooran's girl servant, on her way back from putting out the trash, brought home a curious clump of very pretty feathers. "Look what I found!" she hollered, rushing into the kitchen. In her childish excitement she had forgotten

153

that animals are not welcome in the house, particularly in the kitchen. The children all ran to see what the girl had captured. "It was hobbling on its wings, so easy to catch, . . ." she began.

Aunt Tooran was squatting on the kitchen floor, salting egg-plants for tomorrow's lunch (they would soak up less oil that way). She started up to see what the girl was so eagerly extending toward her. There was a small movement of feathers as the bird turned its head to reveal the face of an owl. Tooran froze halfway up from her squat. Her face paled, her eyes bulged in throbbing terror. She began to scream, "Throw it out, throw it out, get it out of here!"

The terrified servant, not realizing what an awful thing she had been holding, threw the owl on the kitchen floor in a panic. Tooran's screamings became unintelligible. The frightened children scattered out of the kitchen to get help. Tooran screamed and shook as though a demon inside her were being exorcised. Her husband came leaping down the stairs ready for the worst.

When he saw his wife cornered by the bird, he exhaled his alarm and slumped in relief. Then he became angry. "Tooran, I thought someone was strangling you. Who is going to explain to the neighbors tomorrow what the screaming was about? Do you want the children to have nightmares?" He took the bird out, mumbling something about when he was a boy in the village, he used to play with owls all the time. When he came back from throwing the owl in the trash, he berated Tooran for being superstitious, irrational, and hysterical. "An owl is just another bird," he explained, "nothing unlucky about it." Tooran, still shaky and pale, appeared genuinely ashamed and repentant.

The next day, the entire house was scrubbed, starting with the kitchen. All present at last night's scene were sent to the bathhouse where their outer skins were scraped away with pumice. All clothes were boiled and a new trash can was appointed. Nevertheless, a month later Tooran's husband began to feel unusual muscle fatigue. He was quickly diagnosed as having myasthenia gravis and told there was no cure.

Farabi was sure that an old car accident had something to do with it. The doctors could not speculate. Tooran was sure it was the owl.

She was even bold enough to suggest it to a doctor, who ridiculed her. But the doctor had not seen the dying owl keep its face hidden until it was time to show it to Tooran. He had not seen the demon inside Tooran throw a fit. He had not seen the owl's face looking devilishly amused by the joke. So what did the doctor know? Did he have a cure?

Aunt Tooran was not paranoid; she had reason to fear a curse. She had been bad. I had heard people say, "Tooran has worms" (Iranian for "she enjoys tormenting people") or "She is full of broken glass" ("she cannot be trusted"). All of this was true. Tooran's soul profited from trouble. She had a genius for quoting one's most harmless statement in situations where great damage would be done. Like a demolitions expert, she knew exactly where to put the charge to bring the whole structure down. Once, noticing that my mother was getting along too cordially with Aunt Effat, she invited Effat to her house to tell her that my mother was two-faced about her affections. To prove it, she called my mother on the phone and complained bitterly about Effat, bringing up cleverly catalogued and cross-referenced old issues. My mother fell for the trap and sympathized by voicing some of her own complaints—only Tooran was no longer on the phone, she had passed the receiver to Effat. The ensuing hostilities refreshed Tooran greatly.

But her wickedness had a practical side: if ever a conspiracy was needed, Tooran would be called to mastermind it. My mother went to seek her counsel on how to deal with the new servant who refused to go shopping. He was a little boy, Mahmood, whose mother had taught him to pretend ignorance as to the whereabouts of the marketplace. It did no good to show him time after time; his mother had taught him well and my mother was no match for her. The mother worried that her little boy would be lost or run over by a car, but it was exhausting not to be able to send the boy on errands outside the house.

Tooran told my mother to send the boy to the grocery store, telling him that he could also buy himself an ice cream. A decent enough solution except that Tooran called Agha Ali, the grocer, and told him that if Mahmood showed up to buy ice cream, to tell him that they were out of it. Why would Agha Ali agree to such a thing? For someone of Tooran's skills, a coconspirator was as easy to find as a bridge partner.

Tooran had another use for us. She spared nothing in the defense of her relatives against outsiders. Once she gave such a tongue-lashing to one of my teachers, who had been overzealous with the whip, that he stopped whipping his students altogether. But she was just as vicious in defending her immediate family against the rest of the clan. To her, humanity was a structured priority of loyalties. Her allegiances were hard-wired such that it was impossible to override this circuitry of instinct with truth, friendship, beauty, logic, justice, religion, or even magic.

But though she continued to defy the powers that cursed her, it was obvious that the owl incident had somewhat humbled her. For when the mullah with no legs visited her home, that evil, troublemaking spark in her eyes vanished. It was as though the demon inside her had hopped fearfully out of sight of the mullah.

Holding a thick black chador tightly around her face, Tooran had brought up her owl theory with our mullah. He did not profess ignorance of the occult, nor did he wish to encourage inquiry into these matters, but his evasion was satisfying. "The owl is God's creature," he said. "Fear only God and you have nothing to fear."

The mullah with no legs knew how to conquer fear. Farabi often questioned the mullah about the moment of death and the first night in the grave. He suspected the mullah had come very close to dying himself. After their talks, the mullah recited the Koran with a deeply meditative lilt that left behind a cleansed feeling, like a good night's sleep.

The other mullah barked the revealed verses with an enthusiasm and vigor the likes of which I would not encounter until years later in America. He always ended his sessions with this sycophantic reminder of the truce between the clergy and the Shah: "May the Almighty preserve the monarchy and bestow upon our Shah the long life of Noah." This last statement also served to keep the neighbors from complaining about the noise. Although there was a city ordinance forbidding such broadcasts on the pain of the offender's electricity being shut off, no one would dare bring a complaint against a loudspeaker that spoke favorably of the Shah. It was quite possible, they thought, that this was a trap set by the secret police to flush out the malcontents.

The carpenter delighted in all of this. With God and the Shah in his corner, how could he lose? Against all odds, the American chicken business was not doing badly. The Iranian palate complained that the birds did not taste gamey enough and that their eggs were sallow and runny. But despite their unpopularity, these chickens were making slow but stubborn headway into the Iranian chicken market. Iranians often repeated this conversation someone had overheard between a resentful Iranian chicken and an American chicken:

American chicken (boastfully): "My eggs are so much bigger than yours and they sell for so much more. Just look at the size of that egg."

Iranian chicken (snobbishly): "Shoo, shoo, you big white lump. We Iranians don't believe in busting our anuses for money."

Years later, I would write home to explain that it was wrong to malign the American chicken as a class. In county fairs in America I had met an astonishing variety of chickens and realized that "American chicken" as known to Iranians is just a single subvariety of leghorn with a sorrowful history of genetic manipulation and mass imprisonment.

Given the magnitude of anti-American chicken sentiments, I cannot explain why the bird persisted. Clearly a miracle was at work. The logo mullah was gaining the advantage over the mullah with no legs: while the neighbor was slowly getting richer, Farabi was slowly getting sicker. The neighbors were winning the piety war. But Tooran was not an easy opponent. She would demonstrate a tactical versatility I did not think she possessed.

She knew that at the hotel where Farabi was employed, there worked a talented electrician by the name of Torab. Tooran was sure that Torab would be able to build a jamming device that could turn the tables in her war. Torab was in charge of setting up sound and electricals for the hotel's nightly entertainment. It was a luxury hotel that catered to foreigners. Unlike the modern cement hotels that were being poured by the dozens on the chic northern slopes, this old brick hotel lived in the shade of mature sycamores and cypresses in the no-longer-fancy part of town. Because of its humble location, the hotel was never booked solid, but those foreigners who still benefited from the presence of vegetation and suffered from the sight of concrete and whose skins could sense the difference between a cool breeze and mechanically chilled air stayed nowhere else.

These foreigners had inadvertently helped Farabi keep his accounting job long after the disease had made him useless to his employers. We had found a relative in the Ministry of Labor who was in charge of issuing work permits to foreign workers. Since the hotel's international clientele required international entertainment, the hotel needed work permits for foreign talent. The relative had made it clear that business-is-business notwithstanding, no work permits would be issued unless Farabi kept his job. The inequity in the disability insurance regulations had, at least locally, been remedied. Farabi became accountant emeritus with some cut in pay, and an assistant was hired to do the accounting. As part of the settlement, the hotel management had insisted that he show up for work every day.

Very early each morning, Tooran would dress Farabi in suit and tie. Daryoosh, their son, would slowly walk him to the bus station. There the conductor helped him into the crowded bus and cleared a place for him. A special stop was made near the hotel, where Farabi's brother, who also worked at the hotel, took over his care. In the afternoon, Daryoosh waited for him at the bus station to bring him home. Farabi leaned on Daryoosh's arm and took slow shuffling steps. The two had become the other symbiotic pair in the neighborhood. But while the mullah and the plaid seemed to communicate with elbow signals, Daryoosh and his father were always telling stories and laughing. It was hard to imagine what a dying man and his son had to say to each other that was so entertaining. Day after day they could be seen in the streets, one animated, the other limp, and both thoroughly amused.

One day father and son returned bearing Torab's electronic jamming device. The inventor had warned them that the device might not work. It could render useless all the radios and televisions in the neighborhood, but a closed circuit P.A. system would be harder to affect.

For a week before the neighbor's next broadcast Daryoosh had fun jamming Radio Iran. He was ignoring another one of Torab's warnings: for security reasons any unauthorized use of the airwaves was highly illegal. Even owning a walkie-talkie or a remote-control toy could win the offender a tour of SAVAK (the Shah's secret police) facilities. A monstrous hybrid of CIA training and domestic brutality, SAVAK made the KGB look like a petting zoo. But what was worse, if the neighbors found out that it was Daryoosh who had jammed the final episode of a popular mystery, he would have longed for the relative comfort of the SAVAK torture chambers.

That Friday we all sat around Torab's box waiting for the broadcast to start. Daryoosh was not wearing a lab coat and his hair was combed down, but otherwise he was behaving quite like a mad scientist. Sitting at the controls of Torab's box (a single on-off switch), his eyes glowed with Faustian passion. His fingers quivered hesitantly over the switch which, once thrown, would irreversibly transform Life As We Knew It in the neighborhood. Would God permit this? We all wondered.

The broadcast began. The mullah started with a few clever salutations. He was beginning to sound like a disc jockey. Let him warm up, we thought. As long as he spoke Farsi, we listened, giggled, and waited. As soon as he plunged into his imitation Arabic, Tooran nodded meaningfully to Daryoosh who, with historical emphasis, threw the switch.

The crashing sound of hopes being dashed drowned out whatever meager effect Torab's gadget had on the loudspeaker. There was a faint raspberry loud enough perhaps to annoy an audiophile but certainly far too soft to thwart the mullah's sonic rampage. Tooran, disappointed in electronic warfare, left the room heavyhearted. The rest of the household, also in a somber mood, abandoned Daryoosh and went back to mundane existence. Daryoosh, like a believer whose UFO was late, refused to abandon the sham. He sat pawing the gadget mournfully.

About a half hour later, we were all busy doing unmemorable

things when we noticed that something was different. The continuous Arabic had subsided and was replaced by a curious sequence: the mullah said "birthday" loudly and waited. The faint raspberry loud enough to annoy the audiophile followed. The mullah repeated "birthday" and waited. Again the faint raspberry sound. We all rushed to Daryoosh's room. He was on the floor having a seizure of laughter. The mullah's sermon had to do with an imam's birthday, so Daryoosh activated the gadget only after the word "birthday." Religious sermons characteristically feature repeated words, and it was not long before the mullah realized that the word "birthday" caused a funny buzzing in the system. His scientific curiosity aroused, he had temporarily abandoned God and was seeking his own answers to the ways of nature. Tooran was trying to rebuke Daryoosh for his irreverence. It was one thing to jam a loudspeaker, quite another to make light of an imam's birth. Did he want Farabi to get worse? But she could not contain the chuckles that kept bursting through her frowning face. The demon inside her was excitedly peering through her eyeballs, happily waving to get the attention of an offspring it had not known about—the demon inside Daryoosh. This tearful reunion of mother and child demons was touching to see.

Chuckles still percolating through her scowls, Tooran made Daryoosh stop the heresy. She reminded him that this sort of thing could backfire. Not only would it not stop the mullah's broadcasts, it might intensify them. Also, if anyone found out about the mockery, who could stop the angry mob? Certainly the neighbors would put two and two together and realize it was Daryoosh who was jamming their radios and televisions.

Torab's box was returned. He was told that his invention did not work. No mention was made of the use that was made of it. It is probably now forgotten in the dank hotel tool shop, covered by dust and grease. Maybe it is still smarting from the dent inflicted by its disappointed creator, who was never told how marvelously his brainchild had performed. Such is the fate of boxes that mock the Unseen Powers.

Next time the mullah with no legs showed up, Tooran mentioned the broadcasts. Could he persuade his colleague to give up the microphone? The mullah said he had more pull with Allah than with the theological establishment. He would pray for a solution. Why did we not think of this before? It would have saved us many nights of sleepless agony. Miraculously, within a few months after the mullah with no legs started his prayers against the P.A. system, the neighbors moved out. There was much ecstatic revelry. The victorious Tooran set the fruit and vegetableseller to the task of researching the carpenter's downfall so she could gloat over the details.

Though the mullah's prayers quickly rid us of the P.A. system, they were helpless against myasthenia gravis. The disease began to affect Farabi's respiration and he asphyxiated slowly. I remember Farabi fighting for breath in a hospital bed. As a last effort to save him, the doctors had removed his thymus gland. It did not work. He lay in the bed rasping and exchanging jokes with his son. "Mohammad, Jesus and Moses were stranded on an island with Sophia Loren. . . ."

The night before his father's death, Daryoosh pulled out a tiny box from his desk and showed me its contents.

"What is it?" I asked.

"*Kafoor* (camphor)."

"What is it good for?"

"It was secretly taken from the mummies of Egypt. If my father were to eat even a pinhead of this, he would be completely cured."

I was about to ask the obvious question, but his teary eyes pleaded with me to humor him.

"Where did you get it?" I finally asked.

I saw the mullah with no legs seven nights after Farabi's death. He had a larger audience than usual. The clan, numbering perhaps a hundred, had been staying at Tooran's since the death. I knew I would not see the mullah again. I would be leaving to study in the U.S., so I was desperate to find out how the mullah had lost his legs. He never talked about it, and the plaid sitting on the stairs in the hall had resisted my subtle probing for years. I had told him everything, he had told me nothing. He told me he was the mullah's uncle's son on the mother's side; later he told me he was the mullah's aunt's son on the father's side. When I asked him how the mullah had lost his legs, he would say, "I don't know."

When an Iranian says, "I don't know," most of the time he

means, "I don't trust you." He made me do most of the talking. I had told him I had been to England and he seemed most interested. But all he told me about himself could be placed in a joke jigsaw puzzle—none of the pieces seemed to fit. He was consistent in one thing, however. When I first met him, he said he had been carrying the mullah for five years to the month. As the years went by, he never contradicted himself as to the date he entered the mullah's service. The plaid had trusted me in a way by giving me a strong clue. When I was smart enough to piece his clues together, I would be smart enough to be entrusted with the secret.

When I told the plaid I was leaving Iran for the U.S., he decided to take a risk with me and asked if I had ridden in any Rolls Royces in England. I told him that I had.

"Really, did you ride in Rolls Royces a lot over there?" he said as though he would accept anything I said. He was testing me.

"No. Just once."

"When was that?"

Was he fantasizing that someday he would be carrying the mullah in a plaid Rolls? I told him the story over a plate of halvah. Afterwards he asked me if all Rolls Royces had bulletproof windows. Why would he want bulletproof windows on the mullah's Rolls? I said I did not think so.

"The Shah's Rolls Royce has bulletproof windows. Why do you think that is?" he asked. I was jolted. No sane Iranian brought up the Shah in the context of assassination. What was his fantasy leading to? But a jolt was what I needed to put everything together.

I was completely off the mark: this was no fantasy of grandeur. He was leading the horse to water and he had to jolt me into taking a drink. He could not remind me outright of the violent clash between the followers of Khomeini and the forces of the Shah on the fifth of June 1963. On that day, the fifteenth of Khordad 1342 by the Iranian calendar, hundreds of members of the Iranian clergy were rounded up by the secret police. The plaid could not directly tell me that when the mullah was dragged to the SAVAK chambers, he still had his legs. He could not say that, because how did he know I was not one of thousands of SAVAK informers still on the lookout for any remnants of resistance to the Shah? For that matter, how did I know *he* was not a SAVAK informer feeling out how *I* stood on the issues? This dangerous conversation had to be broken off. A little confirmation is not worth risking so much.

That afternoon I went upstairs to tell Tooran why I thought the mullah had lost his legs and why the mullah never sent blessings after the Shah.

With all the relatives around, it had been a hectic seven days. There had been much cooking, many children, plenty of fights, and much weeping. Tonight Farabi's soul would ascend to heaven. After tonight, Tooran would be left alone to grieve. But now, in the afternoon heat, the guests were all napping.

I found Tooran sobbing in Farabi's empty closet. The clothes had been given away to charity, but the closet still smelled like him. I thought I would wait for a better time to talk to her about the mullah. For a few minutes, I watched her mourn in a rocking huddle, then left quietly without being seen. By the time a better opportunity arose to talk to Tooran, I had decided to keep the secret. It would not have been good for the mullah's business if people feared they were associating with a dissident. I almost betrayed the plaid; I certainly would have if Whatever Protects Us had not kept my mouth shut long enough for me to become a little bit more Iranian.

With Farabi gone and the logo mullah no longer keeping our ears busy, the neighborhood felt lonely. I missed the logo mullah; he pumped energy into the community. I have since wondered if it was not his energy that kept Farabi alive. I am sure the carpenter's wife would not resent our benefiting from the spillover from her mullah, especially if she knew what a great debt she owed Tooran.

The fruit and vegetableseller filled in the details. A few months after the mullah with no legs agreed to pray for a solution to the P.A. problem, the carpenter had a windfall and bought a luxurious house on the cooler foothills of north Tehran. While the logo mullah's prayers had helped only to keep the chickens alive, the mullah with no legs made the business take off overnight. The carpenter imported a technique for making chickens lay eggs with two yolks inside. The double-yolk egg is considered a sign of luck among Iranians, so the carpenter became a very successful egg merchant. I had a hunch our mullah was better than their mullah, but the way this superiority was confirmed left us feeling cheated. Was it Allah's infinite wisdom or just a devilish prank? I have it on my list of things to ask when *I* meet the Almighty.

That summer I left for the United States. It was a lonely departure with none of the usual fuss over the traveler. My father was going through one of his isolationist phases and did not want to have anything to do with the relatives. He would not tell anyone my departure date. I did not want a ceremonial good-bye myself because I felt bad about leaving so soon after I had been released from my high school prison. There was a literacy corps in Iran at the time that could serve as a substitute for military service. I wanted to volunteer for one of those villages accessible only by mule. For a while at least, I wished to step out of my middle-class timetable. The clan condemned me for acting like a spoiled teenager. Aunt Tooran reminded me of the millions of Iranian youth who would give an eye for the opportunity I was getting. How could I arrogate to myself the right to spurn such a prize? She was right; it was morally safer to go. Once in the U.S., however, I met an Iranian who should have followed his heart.

The Prodigy

I met Hadi in the second year of my stay in the U.S. He was reluctant to accept my request to play his music for us, and it took several meetings to convince him that I was not there to recruit him for our group. We were a loose association of homesick Iranian students who met weekly on the pretense of political activity. This activity consisted mainly of reading books that had been banned in Iran and sharing mildly reformist opinions. A few days before I came to the U.S., I was invited by SAVAK to spy on this group. The SAVAK man's approach was indirect. He told me that I could participate in Iranian political activity abroad if I wished; but in order to avoid misunderstanding, I should send him short reports explaining the reason for my presence as well as a brief summary of who said what. I was assured that if my reports were of high enough quality, I would be compensated.

165

Given the paucity of detail and the briefness of the meeting, I took this to be more of a warning than an invitation. Two more send-off warnings came from the education ministry: (1) return once you have your degree, your education belongs to the country; (2) do not cause trouble for your family by participating in political activity abroad, there are SAVAK agents everywhere.

Hadi probably received the same threats and wisely did not wish to be involved with subversive groups. Maybe there were some organizations that deserved serious concern, but surely our gatherings could only be healthy for the country. The political discourse and exchange of ideas were badly needed. It was state-induced claustrophobia that eventually transformed tongue and brain into tooth and claw.

When I told Hadi about my meeting with the SAVAK man, he recounted a similar experience. SAVAK had also advised him to stay away from politically active women, as they had V.D. We laughed over this. I told him that now I understood his reluctance, I could do something about it. If he came to our meeting and played his music for us home-starved Iranians, I would persuade the women to ignore him. A few laughs later he agreed to come.

Hadi did not look like a person that played the tar. He was too young. Tar players are left to mature on the vines of experience until they are bald and broken. They often resemble their instrument. The shiny bald head nodding over the big belly mirrors the double-gourd construction. The rows of gold and silver caps glittering over decaying teeth sympathize visually with the brass and steel strings stretched over the ivory-inlaid fret board. Tars and their players smell of mulberry wood and musician sweat. But with his short, orderly and compact appearance, Hadi looked more like a harmonica than a tar.

Nevertheless, when he slumped over his tar and took command of the mystic forces of the instrument, the young boy vanished. The polyester shirt and pants became the woolen garb of the Sufi. His short hair grew wild and mysterious over a face wrinkled with wisdom. His playing stirred and melted us like sugar in hot coffee. The aroma of mulberry wood that surrounded him was that of the live tree. His tar grew roots and leaves, spread itself in the sunny breeze and sang of furious love for the land that grew it. He did not play accurately. His fingers tangled during the fast passages and sometimes the notes were slurred, but even the errors added to the sense of depth, like the fallen stones of a ruined palace.

I visited Hadi often, mostly to persuade him to play his tar, but he seldom obliged. Most of our time together was spent chatting over tea and chess. Soon I realized that he was an undefeatable chess player. The few instances when I gained the upper hand I attribute to his diplomacy. I did not mind being beaten by him, although normally my defeatsmanship is quite puerile. He had no pride with which to scrape a delicate ego. I was allowed to take my moves back as often and as far back as I wished; he enjoyed my desire to turn back the clock and live my chess life over. The lesson: if God is like Hadi, it makes no difference; the play is governed by something other than just the permutations of moves. Once I asked him why he traded queens so early in the game.

"The queen's versatility is not worth its unpredictability. It can win or lose the game too easily," he said.

"What do you consider to be the most important piece?" I asked.

"The pawn."

"You mean because there are so many of them?"

"There is only one pawn; it occupies eight spaces. If you think of your pawns as separate entities, then you will use them that way and lose the game."

Hadi was artist, philosopher and mystic—with a very odd hobby. He had a passion for guns. Sometimes he took me to a nearby store to show me their gun selection and ask my advice on which gun to buy. I asked him what he needed the gun for. He said target practice. I recommended a pebble and a coke can.

As long as I knew him, he did not buy a gun. But he had an American friend who owned many guns, and they often went to the range together. One weekend Hadi invited me to join them.

"Hadi, you are not in the military and you buy your meat at the supermarket." I asked in criticism, "Why do you need target practice?"

"It is not really practice," he said.

"What then? You enjoy the noise?"

He thought for a while. "Yes, it slaps you in the face." He laughed and added, "The kick, also the kick."

"What do you imagine your targets to be?" I said, getting to the point.

"*Vozkakhs.*"

"What?"

"Frogs. People from the Gilan region call them vozakhs. My targets are giant vozakhs the size of people."

"I did not know you were from the Gilan region. You have a Tehrani accent."

"I will tell you the story later," he said.

Target practice was a misnomer for what Hadi did. He did not need practice. He did not seem even to aim. It was as though the bullet was in the target even before he pulled the trigger. All that noise and mechanical energy was just an afterthought. His American friend raved with praise, but I worried about the terribly sad face Hadi wore when he fired the weapon. I avoided the temptation to ask him about it until later when guns were not present.

But the next time I visited him, I found him busy with another idea. He was frustrated that the washing machines at the laundromat did not automatically put in the right amount of soap. It seemed unreasonable that the automation would stop short of this obvious step. "You get an 'A' for logic and an 'F' for anthropology," I said.

"How is that?" he asked defensively.

"The brand of soap is very important to Americans. Don't you watch TV? One can't put just any soap in the machine. The soap has to be suited to one's character."

"So we put in a lever that selects the right soap," he suggested.

"By 'soap' they mean the package, not the contents." I said.

"You like to exaggerate, but I know Americans like to open packages. I think that is why they give each other so many presents."

"They give presents because they are generous and friendly. I think it is a good national habit."

"Since you know so much about Americans, there is something you can help me with," he said. The laundromat was only the approach. Now came the real question.

"There is a girl," he confided.

"In one of your classes?"

"Yes."

"American?"

"Of course," he said impatiently. Don't waste time asking what you already know, I reminded myself.

"Well, what about her?" I asked. He stared. "You are in love with her and she ignores you. You wish to know how to get her attention." He smiled. I asked him what he had done so far.

"I asked Goodarz for advice. He gets a lot of girls, and he said I should tell her I am Italian. American girls like Italian men."

"They like French men better," I noted.

"But I don't speak any French."

"You know Italian?" I asked, surprised. He looked disappointedly at me.

"No, but neither do the girls. They all know a little French, though."

"Very clever," I said, disgusted with Goodarz. "So she thinks you are from Italy? I think you have created a major problem for yourself."

"I have not even talked to her yet. Don't jump to conclusions," he said irritably. I can't read your mind, Hadi, I thought to myself. First you want me to jump to conclusions, then you don't want me to jump to conclusions.

"If you have not talked to her, then how do you know you like her?"

"If you have never fallen in love with a woman just by the way she looks, then you must be a homo."

"Quite the contrary, professor. Before I fall in love with anyone, I at least ascertain her gender by talking to her," I chided.

"If she has gone through such trouble to confuse her gender, I would not take her word for it. Do be cautious," he counselled.

"Have you at least heard her speak?" I asked.

"Yes, she has a fine voice."

"What did she say?"

"I don't remember. She might have said 'arctangent of alpha is thirty degrees.'"

"Was it?" I pressed.

"Was it what?"

"Thirty degrees."

"Enough joking," Hadi said. "What difference does it make how many degrees it was?"

"I mean, is she smart?"

"Look, don't try to prove to me that I do not love her. I am very clear about that. I just need to get her to notice me."

"What are your intentions with her?" I asked.

"It depends on whether or not she is a virgin."

"She is probably not."

"How can you be so sure? Were you there?" He was getting testier.

"Falling in love with a stranger has its price. She is probably not a virgin" I insisted arrogantly.

"Then I will want her for a girlfriend."

"Don't tell her you are worried about her virginity. It is not a good opening line."

"What is a good line that will make her notice me?" he asked boyishly.

"The Americans have an expression—'tall, dark and handsome.' You are not tall, but you are dark and handsome twice over. I am sure she has noticed you already." He seemed very encouraged by the compliment.

"She has a boyfriend," he announced. He was giving me the problem bit by bit.

"What is he like?"

"Football player. He sits next to her in class. She lives in a sorority." He knew more about her than he had admitted at first. I suggested that he make friends with her and wait in line. Besides, it would be easier for him to approach her if his intentions were social.

"But I want her now," he stressed. He had stopped listening to me, and I was angry. Strangely, I was angry at her too.

"Then Italian is not going to help. Tell her you are a med student and keep yourself vulnerable to marriage."

"That is immoral. I would never deceive a woman that way."

"But you would tell her you are Italian."

"That is different. There is a difference between a liar and one whose mother is a whore (i.e., a bastard). I will lie, but I will not make a whore out of my mother. It is chauvinistic to think just because she lives in a sorority that she wants to marry a doctor."

"I am sorry. I did not wish to belittle her. Obviously, you have strong feelings," I said.

170

"What can I do that is honorable?" he said with resignation. I was tempted to say, "Why don't you put on a cowboy hat and show her you can shoot the nose off a mosquito at a hundred yards," but I thought he would interpret that as yet another jab at her character.

Finally I said, "Invite her to one of our cultural meetings and play your tar for her." Even though medical degrees were rapidly replacing serenades in contemporary romantic literature, it was the best advice I could give.

Several weeks later, I caught him late at night cozied in a booth at the students' cafeteria. He was sipping tea in front of a chessboard. A cigarette butt smoldered in the ashtray across from him. He did not smoke; his opponent had left him. I scanned the chessboard. Hadi was in terrible shape. Checkmate seemed imminent.

"Hey, professor, looks like you found your match," I said. He looked up, happy to see me.

"No, you homo, the bugger gave up. I am just seeing if there is anything he could have done." Then his eyes lit up with an idea. He offered me the winning side.

It was dark and rainy outside. The large picture windows crawled with the sinuous meanderings of raindrops. Somewhere beyond, out in the cold, another Hadi and I playing chess permeated the dripping bushes. The clanging of doors being locked signaled us to wrap up the game. He was winning anyway.

"Come to my house and I will steam some Persian tea," he said.

We helped each other into our coats, tucked up the collars, and pushed through the door into the wind.

"Tell me what happened with the girl," I said, avoiding a puddle.

"I invited her to hear me play my tar."

"Did she accept?"

"She asked me what a tar was and I explained. She said, 'Sort of like an Arabian guitar?' I said, 'No.'"

"Then what?" I pursued.

"Then she smiled politely and said she didn't think she would be interested. I explained that she need not think of this as a date—there would be others present that she could meet, but she said her boyfriend would not like that. You know what her boyfriend studies? I found out."

"Premed," I said.

"Sometimes your guesses are lucky. Besides, half the school is premed. How do you know she does not really love him?"

"She turned down a private performance by the world's greatest musician, called you an Arab guitarist. And you ask me why I think she is after his medical degree? Why do you still defend her?"

"It is not only her. I take my tar to the river sometimes and play under the trees. But the river does not understand and the trees are bored. I just sound bad. It is not the musician that makes the music— it is not even the tar. We just make the noise."

"Who makes the music?" I asked.

"The land where the mulberry tree grew."

We reached his apartment cold and soaked. He turned up the heat and started the tea. I wriggled into a beanbag and stuck my wet toes in the heater grill.

"Do you know how long I had played the tar when you first heard me play?" he asked from the kitchen.

"Ten years," I guessed.

"Three months."

I bolted up, astonished. I calculated that he had already been in the U.S. for two months when he first played for us. That left him only one month to study in Iran.

"Why did you not start earlier?" I lamented.

"I wanted to, but my father would not let me. He bought me the tar as a going-away present."

"Why didn't he let you?"

"My father blames my uncle, but it is the fault of the entire family. They were all against it, including my father."

He brought the tea, Iranian-style: silver tray, dainty saucers and glasses, lump sugar. The china teapot sat on top of the samovar in the kitchen. He had bought the samovar and the tea set in Los Angeles. He continued with his story.

"When I was eight years old, my cousin bought a tar. He took lessons and played at the family gatherings. We have some very good singers in the family and my cousin accompanied them. We also have good drummers that accompanied the tar. I enjoyed my cousin's play- ing very much. I had been listening to the tar on the radio all my life,

172

but hearing it live was something different. Do you remember the mattress beaters yelling in the streets carrying those funny bows?" he asked.

"They came to your house and fluffed up the cotton in your mattresses?" I reminisced.

"Yes, they tore open the mattress and pulled the cotton out. Then they thwacked the bowstring over the cotton to fluff it up. I used to take the man a bowl of ice water, then stay and listen to the zinging and the piffing and the thwacking for hours."

"Yes, I remember being fascinated by the cotton leaping and dancing to the music of the bow," I said.

He continued, "When I heard the live tar, it was like the stuffy cotton in my spirit was pulled out and fluffed up. After my cousin had put the tar away in the other room, I used to sneak in and make sounds on it. My cousin caught me several times and took it away, chiding that the tar was not a toy. But one day he noticed the evenness of my tremolo. He was impressed and he let me play his tar when he came over. I started pestering my parents for one. They said they worried it would affect my studies. They argued that if I had time, I should use it to improve my math grades. You remember how important it was to get good math grades?"

"Yes," I said "you could flunk anything, but as long as you got good math grades, you were forgiven. But you could be a genius in the arts and no one would ask after you."

"A revolting attitude. The country will suffer for it," he said.

"The country needs to catch up technologically." I reminded him.

"At what expense? You know they don't even let you go abroad and study music because they do not wish to waste precious foreign currency on something the country does not need?"

I said, "I did not know that, but why go abroad to study Persian music?"

"Don't be dense, it is the attitude I am angry about. Tell someone you are an engineer and you get respect, tell him you are a tar player and it is like you told him you are a whore. That is what my father told me: 'Do you want to grow up to be a *motreb*?' The very word motreb, what does it mean?"

"Musician," I said.

"No, it means giver of pleasure. Like a whore. A good musician exposes his most private feelings to the public. How is that different from a whore selling her private parts? My father used to stop in front of street musicians shaming themselves for money and tell me to imagine myself in the future doing the same thing."

"But, Hadi, you are no ordinary musician. Besides, there are lots of music classes in Iran and people enroll without being ashamed."

"Of course, it is all right to dabble. It is quite a status symbol to be able to play at gatherings. People love good music—they do not settle for less—but no one wants his son to grow up to be a tar player."

"I know," I said, sincerely sympathetic.

"My cousin pleaded for me and vouched that my grades would not drop if I bought a tar and took lessons. But my father would not give in. I went on strike and stopped doing my homework. The beatings did no good. I promised I would fail that year if I was not allowed to study tar. This convinced them even more that I was willing to sacrifice my future for the sake of the tar. Finally, my father said he would bring it up with my uncle who is older and whose wisdom can be trusted."

"Your uncle said 'No'?"

"He said he had a friend who is brother to a tar master. He would arrange for a session with the master to test and see if I should pursue the tar."

"The tar master said you were no good?" I exclaimed unbelievingly.

"I will bring more tea," he said, and left for the kitchen.

"Tell me the truth, the tar master said you were no good?" I yelled to the kitchen.

He brought the tea and finished his story. When he was done, I also knew why he was such a good shot.

I walked home through the drip drip of drooling rain gutters. The serenity of the quietly weeping trees was interrupted only once by a motorcycle that sounded like it was blowing its nose. "What a waste," was all I could feel.

The tar master's brother lived in the province of Gilan in the Caspian region. Gilan has three colors: sea blue, sky grey, and leaf green. Where there is not rice or tea fields, there is forest. Here people live in a water-abundant culture. The trees and shrubbery break up the spaces, providing natural privacy; the high brick walls of the desert architecture give way to hedges, reeds, and bamboo. Wildlife is so abundant that in the right season unwary reptiles and amphibians can be seen flapping on the road surface by the hundreds.

Hadi, his father, and his uncle arrived a day earlier than the tar master. It was polite not to appear to be on business. The uncle and the tar master's brother were school friends. The reunion was full of joy and reminiscences. There was broiled lamb, local delicacies, much vodka, and great merriment. The uncle was concerned about his friend. Why didn't he transfer to the capital, there is more civilization there: did he not worry that his two sons would grow up with a Gilani accent?

The sons were about Hadi's age—one slightly younger, one slightly older. They were very hospitable and wanted to make sure Hadi was enjoying himself. They talked about movies, played cards, and made lemonade. At dusk, they invited him to go to the marsh with them. Hadi was curious about the marsh; they are rare south of the Alborz mountains.

"Dusk is a good time," the boys said. "The vozakhs come out."

"The what?"

"Vozakhs. You call them frogs," one said.

"And they are sluggish this time of day so we can shoot them with our air guns," said the other.

"You eat frogs here?" Hadi asked, remembering the strange food he had eaten.

"No," they laughed, "we shoot them for target practice." This was hunting country and the inhabitants learned to hunt early. Hadi said he would go to watch, but he would not shoot any frogs.

"Just as well," they said, "we only have two guns anyway."

As promised, the marsh was full of frogs. The boys were not skilled killers though. They made too much noise and scared away a lot of the frogs within range. The ones that stayed were mostly spared by bad aim. Nevertheless, they shot enough frogs to revolt Hadi.

"When they got hit, they leaped vertically up in the air so that their white bellies flashed in the dusk. Sometimes the shot had gone through and you could see dark fluid oozing out of the hole in the soft belly." Hadi begged them to stop but the boys were having a good day and mocked him for acting like a city boy. They were home by dinnertime, but Hadi could not eat. He went straight to bed and had frog nightmares all night.

The next day the tar master showed up. He was old, fat, and balding. "He looked like a man with a lot of debts," Hadi said.

After tea and amenities, the tar master was told that Hadi's uncle was a superb singer. The tar master's brother brought out the *doonbak* (drum), and the three of them turned some very nice classic poetry into music. Once they were done, the tar master half patronizingly asked Hadi if he recognized the system they had played in. The boy confidently identified the system as *Shur* (ecstasy).

"Excellent!" said the tar master, surprised. "How old did you say you were?"

"Nine," Hadi said.

"You have good ears for such a young boy. But Shur is not for children. It will wilt a young soul. It takes maturity to avoid depression."

"What is a good system for children?" Hadi asked. The tar master was stuck; he did not wish to belittle any system by recommending it for children.

"One usually starts with *Mahoor* these days," he said finally. "Did you bring your tar?"

"I do not have a tar yet. You are supposed to test and see if I am any good."

The tar master laughed and looked in the direction of Hadi's embarrassed kin. "Repeat after me," he said as he played the opening phrase of the preface to Mahoor. The boy repeated the phrase perfectly with his voice.

"Now play it on the tar," said the tar master, handing Hadi the tar. Awkwardly the boy hugged the heavy gourds and barely reaching, adjusted one of the tuning keys slightly. The tar master was amused by the unintended insult. He hummed the phrase to refresh the boy's memory. Hadi played the proud opening declaration loudly and assertively but, to the amazement of all present, continued over the next few minutes to complete the entire preface to Mahoor.

176

"Where did he learn this?" the tar master asked Hadi's father.

"I don't know, I don't know," said the proud and flustered father.

"I heard it on the radio," Hadi said, "the day they manured the garden."

The curious tar master had the boy play other things the radio had taught him and said finally, "The boy has aptitude."

Hadi was beside himself. After all the fights and the beatings and the rebukes, this was a major victory. He beamed proudly at his vanquished kin, who sat fidgeting uncomfortably.

"Too much aptitude," the tar master warned. "If at this age he understands Shur, he will not just practice for fun. He will become obsessed and abandon everything for the sake of his music."

"Do you think it is wise to get him a tar?" Hadi's father asked. He wanted a definitive yes or no.

"It is up to you. All I can determine is that he will grow up to be a great tar player but will not amount to anything else. How are his grades in school?"

"He does well. He is very good in math," Hadi's father said.

Hadi was dumbfounded. "I swear, I swear, I will not become obsessed," he pleaded. "I will only practice a half hour a day."

"Boy," said the tar master sadly, "they tell me you have a head for figures. If you were failing in school, I would say 'all right, the boy has nothing else going for him, at least let him grow up to be a poor musician.' But you have a future, a good brain, a good father who cares for you despite how you feel about him now. Why throw all this away? Someday you will find a good woman and you can give *her* all the love you have for the tar."

"I promise I will not become obsessed," Hadi pleaded, tears on his cheeks.

"You are already obsessed, see how you listen to the radio? You are the moth, the tar is the flame; you will burn," he said.

"Then why did you become a tar player?"

"I was not good for anything else," the master said sadly. "I failed school."

At dusk, Hadi asked the brothers if he could go to the marsh with them.

"Want to shoot some vozakhs?" the boys asked excitedly.

"Bring plenty of pellets," Hadi told them.

He wanted to see the bleeding hole in the belly; it was not enough to shoot them, he had to get them at the right spot so the pellet would go through. He loaded and fired tirelessly, never missing. The brothers saw no more frogs, but Hadi spotted them—camouflaged, hidden, buried, it did not matter. Hadi found them and shot them until the surface of the pond was crowded with the white of bloated frog bellies and the boys would give him no more pellets.

Hadi was sweaty and trembling as he remembered the massacre. I thought I would change the subject. I asked him how he finally got his tar.

"It was a going-away present. I stopped nagging my father for it after the session with the tar master, but he remembered. He said someday I would return to Iran a famous scientist—just think how much more admiration I would get if it were known that I also felt it was important to keep our musical traditions alive."

"But was he not worried that you would not study if you had a tar?"

"Who will listen to me here? There is no nourishment here for the kind of music I play. I would starve. My father knew that."

"He has great foresight," I said.

"No, he is very stupid. The whole country is stupid. You know those signs they put in restaurant windows 'No shoes, no shirt, no service?'"

"Yes" I said.

"Well, 'No arts, no music, no science.'"

* * *

One day I saw a woman in the park picking leaves off a small tree. Curious, I went over to ask if she raised silkworms. I had found a mulberry tree. I called Hadi to tell him about it but he said he had sold his tar for $94.75. It was like he told me someone I knew had died. I was very sad and rebuked him viciously. Later I asked him about the strange price. He said he had not really sold the tar. He had bashed it against his apartment wall, costing himself $94.75 in penalties against his rental deposit.

Many of Iran's finest musicians left the country after the revolution. Some of them found a haven in Los Angeles, where a large Iranian community nurtures our traditional arts. I hear that Iranian artisans in L.A. are crafting excellent tars using wood from California trees.

Exposure to American culture did not soften Hadi's resignation to his fate. I had hoped the newness of his surroundings would allow him to see that life can be different in ways we cannot imagine. But when his parents came to visit him in the U.S. and I saw the unusually tight bond of tradition among the family members, I could see Hadi's dilemma. Rebelliousness is anathema to a family whose roots go that deep in the soil of tradition. Last I knew, Hadi was back in Iran helping with the family coal business.

I met another Iranian in the U.S. who had also grown up in a family with orthodox views. This friend, however, had made a career out of rebellion. He did not rebel against his parents; he challenged far more formidable authority figures. He was a revolutionary.

The Martyr

Sitting in Kamyar's car was like attending a Sunday sermon. The buttons on his car radio were preset to the Los Angeles Christian stations, and the volume control was cranked most of the way up. His friends used to tease him by suggesting he take out the bucket seats and put in pews. "It's hard to kneel with your seat belt on," was his straight-faced response.

When the strangeness finally wore off, I asked him seriously, "Kamyar, isn't it odd that an avowed Communist such as yourself listens to nothing but Christian broadcasts?"

Kamyar waited until we had exited the freeway and stopped for a red light. Then he said briefly, "I don't listen to everything, like those awful country bands and their twangy Jesus songs. I just listen to the sermons and the speeches."

"I've noticed you switch stations as soon as the music comes on, but what is it about Christ that could fascinate an atheist?"

"Oh, nothing," he shooed away the thought. "I don't listen to the words, just the intonations."

"It's green," I said.

"What's green?"

"The light. You can go now."

"Oh."

He drove until we came to another red light. Then he spoke again.

"When you speak with one person, you sound different than when you talk to ten people. If there are a million people listening, the rhythm and inflection pick up a really nice sweeping effect. It doesn't matter what is being said."

"So you listen to the intonations and fill in your own words?" I guessed.

"Yes," he admitted.

"What words do you put in? Down with imperialism and all that?"

"No, I pretend it is my eulogy," he answered casually. He seemed very sincere.

A few more red lights went by while I composed my next question. "Do you imagine that you could hear your own eulogy after you die?"

"You mean my spirit coming back to listen?"

"Yes."

"There is no life after death, only eulogies. Christ's resurrection is just a metaphor for that great eulogy known as Christianity."

So much for the theory that Kamyar was secretly religious.

We reached our destination, an old basketball court temporarily converted to an arena for yelling out political boos and cheers. Ever since Kamyar had moved into the apartment next door to mine earlier that fall, he had been taking me to these debates and rally sessions. We did not have a serious parliament in Iran during the Shah's regime and these gatherings held in the United States by the various Iranian revolutionary groups were the closest thing we had to a congressional debate. We could not pass any laws and had no power to enforce policy, but with a bit of free speech borrowed from our host country, we tried to fashion new ideas for our own.

The speaker's feeble voice, muffled by the throngs, could barely be heard. I could not tell if he was speaking in Farsi or English. But Kamyar was apparently picking up every word. Several times he rose in rabid objection to whatever was being said.

". . . blood of the martyrs . . . bare our chests to the bullets of . . . raze the bastions of oppression . . . last drop of . . . ," Kamyar foamed, as those in his camp applauded and those in the other camps jeered. He spoke as though a war were raging inside him. One could sense the explosions and the rat-tat-tat of machine guns. Millions were extinguished when he screamed "martyr."

While he blasted away, I scanned the overheated room for familiar faces. I found Carol transfixed by the Armageddon staged before her. I had known her for a few years now. Whenever anti-Americans needed American sympathizers, Carol could be counted on. But despite her loyalty and generosity, she was not given much respect by her peers. She sought her friends and lovers among the radical Chileans, Native-Americans, Salvadorans, and Palestinians, who found in her a willing kicking board, masochistically taking the blows for America. If Kamyar wanted a grand eulogy, this kind and righteous woman would settle for a short epitaph: America, Carol died for your sins.

When Carol and I first met, she mistook me for a radical activist. I used to seek the company of political dissenters in the hope of finding something worth committing to. They seemed so certain of their truth that I could not resist finding out what they had to say. When Carol was present, I affected a less neutral reason for my interest in politics. She had a way of making one dramatize one's political concerns. At any rate, since our friendship was made before I disappointed her, I stayed among her circle of friends. Strangely, in her mind, I was the idealist and she the pragmatist.

"There's no such thing as a perfect idea that will make saints out of everybody that follows it. Don't give me any excuses about having doubts. When things are this bad, you have to grab anything that's even a little bit OK and believe in it like it was really really true," she used to say. "So don't just sit there waiting for the Messiah, do something to help make things right."

"So who do you want me to kidnap?"

"Oh, shut up."

She literally fumed as she spoke. I was always fanning away her smoke and dodging her burning cigarettes as she flailed her arms carelessly to emphasize her points.

This was Carol's heyday as a radical sympathizer. The Iranian revolution was around the corner, and anti-American blows were flying left and right. Even though no one could see around the corner and be sure the revolution was coming, clearly something big was about to happen. The various groups of Iranians were quickly uniting against the common enemy, while at the same time making sure their identity was not lost. Each group—the Marxists, the Islamists, the Islamist Marxists, the reformists—was putting out copious amounts of literature defining themselves to each other and establishing a claim to the spoils of the would-be revolution.

Kamyar did not want a revolution. Not yet. He felt the capitalists were rushing matters so as to undermine the Marxists' revolutionary timetable.

"Why else would they (the West) take Khomeini from his obscure exile in Iraq and stick him in Paris where their media crawls all over him like ants on a broken honey jar?" he argued.

"Why would they want Khomeini over the Shah? Khomeini hates Americans," I said.

"You are as naive as the American public. America knows it can't fight any more Vietnams. It needs indigenous anticommunists with popular support. Distasteful as he may seem, Khomeini looks to American policymakers like an ounce of prevention." He continued to lecture me all the way back home from the meeting.

A few days later I found Carol in the student cafeteria. I wanted to say hello and hear what she had to say about the meeting, but she had something else in mind.

"Who was that fiery man you were with the other day?"

"What fiery . . . oh, you mean Kamyar?"

"Is that his name?"

"Don't mind him, he is just a boy."

"He didn't sound like a boy. He knew what he was talking about," she said knowingly.

"Don't waste your time with him. His only interest, and I mean *only*, is radical politics."

"What is he doing hanging around a bourgeois like you then?"

I ignored the jab. "I live next door to him. Whatever our differences, we are both Iranians you know."

"I thought Iranians didn't know how to disagree peacefully."

"So who's disagreeing? He talks, I listen."

"You hypocrite," she muttered, lighting a match. "You know I haven't visited your place in a long time."

"You're telling me? Why did you stop coming?"

She put the match to her cigarette. "I got frustrated," she said, shaking out the flame. "You just don't care what happens to oppressed people."

"You're worse than those Jesus freaks," I complained. "Always trying to recruit me to the causes you pick up from your boyfriends. I feel as if you don't listen except to try to find an opening in my defenses."

"Maybe I should keep trying. Will you be home this afternoon?" she asked alluringly.

"I'll be home, but I can't promise Kamyar will be there."

"I'll just have to chance it then, you jealous boy." She laughed.

"Me? Jealous? Maybe if you stopped smoking." Her cigarette glowed a bright red as she willfully sucked an inch off it. I ran out before she exhaled.

A few months after Carol and Kamyar met, I saw Carol clawing her face in need of a cigarette. She had gained a little weight. Kamyar had ordered her to quit smoking.

"Are you jealous yet?" she said.

"Yes, now please go back to smoking until you quit for *my* sake."

"Kamyar never smokes," she said. I never smoked either, but she was never so proud of *me*.

"I know. He doesn't listen to music either, or go to the movies, or walk on the beach. Just curious, have you corrupted him with sex yet?"

"Our relationship is *not* sexual," she said forcefully.

"That's what I thought. That guy is afraid if he has any fun he may not want to die anymore."

"To fight and die for a good cause is the most noble accomplishment for a human." It sounded like Kamyar.

"Why do you really think he needs so badly to die?" I asked.

"You sound as though he's suicidal. He is not. He just realizes that he has to do what he has to do and he is not going to let fear of death keep him from doing it."

"That is romantic, but really, don't you worry for him, especially these days?"

"*Really*, I do worry about him," she said angrily. "I would explain it to you, but for you, so much commitment is hard to visualize."

"He may be committed, but I don't think he is thinking about it. His bravery is ill-considered. Carol, the revolution in Iran is not a protest demonstration. We're not talking civil disobedience where you get arrested and fingerprinted and then go have a big party."

"Don't patronize me," she snapped, the venom of nicotine withdrawal in her voice. "I know perfectly well what is going on."

What was going on? The Shah had been forced to leave the country, and the revolution had been won with relatively little bloodshed. The repression I had experienced in Iran had led me to believe that any uprising would lead to a bloodbath. That the Shah was not able to convince his powerful army to quell the uprising surprised everyone except Kamyar, who saw it as further evidence that the West had abandoned its puppet.

There was an atmosphere of cautious revelry among the Iranians. The disparate groups that had banded together against the beast were still coexisting democratically. Iranians with ideas as to what Iran should do no longer had any excuse for staying in the U.S. Their ideas were needed at home. If there was to be a democracy in Iran, strong and vigorous political parties were necessary. Ironically, none of the strongest groups were serious about a democracy. Each was cautiously humoring the situation, preparing for the inevitable.

It was around this time that Kamyar decided to go back to Iran.

"There is opportunity for work," he said proudly. He did not mean he had found a job; he meant political work.

"Is work possible now? I hear people are crazy about Khomeini and getting crazier," I cautioned.

"Work is possible," he said with ominous reassurance.

"Have you told Carol?"

He and Carol were a lot closer now. He did not wish to give his comrades the impression that he was less than ascetic, but it was clear that the friendship was progressing. He had told Carol about going back and Carol had offered to follow him.

I told Carol she was crazy. "You haven't known him for that long, and you don't know anything about Iran."

"There you go, patronizing me again. I know what I'm doing," Carol said.

"Have you told him about your stocks?" I asked. Her parents were quite wealthy and had promised to give her a substantial chunk of stocks once she turned twenty-one. They had not mentioned any preconditions as to her political leanings, but apparently the preconditions were implicit. Carol had been denied the promised wealth.

"What stocks? They didn't give me any," she protested.

"What would be the use? You would just give them away." I was flattering her; privately, I felt that the quickest way to change her politics would be to give her the stocks. "Anyway, I don't think it would do any harm to tell him. His parents are rich, too," I said.

"I know," she nodded. "But it didn't help when they took his brother away."

"What brother? He didn't tell me anything about a brother."

"See? I know him a lot better than you think," she said gleefully. Kamyar and I had held many conversations. He did not like to talk much about everyday things; he preferred to talk about "real issues." Nevertheless, he had incidentally revealed quite a bit about his background. The sudden appearance of a brother in the picture puzzled me as to why he had avoided such a harmless topic.

"Who took his brother away?" I asked.

Carol revealed to my astonishment that Kamyar's older brother had been killed by the Iranian secret police many years before. His parents had been very distraught. As good Moslems they could not even understand the godless ideology for which their son had given his life. The mother was still holding monthly commemorations for her fallen child. I could imagine how Kamyar would be affected by this perpetual funeral. I could also see why he would divert our conversations from such a mine field of emotions. Marxist-Leninists are

186

bound by their creed to downplay their personal sufferings in recognition of the greater social pains.

After the death of his brother, Kamyar must have sat through many family *rowzehs*, where the mullah is invited to recite to a weeping audience the emotional story of the martyrdom of Imam Hossein. Hossein, the Prophet's brave grandson, had challenged the Islamic establishment that followed the Prophet's death. His small army of revolutionaries was surrounded by a much superior force, but he went into battle, knowing he would not survive. Oddly, he had taken along his wife and children, the tale of whose sufferings added to the sense of catastrophe masterfully conjured by the mullah.

I remember feeling touched when, after a hot afternoon soccer game, Kamyar had insisted on sharing the bottle of water Carol had brought him. Imam Hossein was denied water by his captors before he was beheaded. For this reason Iranians are careful to share their water. On the anniversary of Hossein's death, tanks of water are placed in the streets so no one goes thirsty. Communist or not, Kamyar was Shiite in upbringing.

Carol was at first eager to follow Kamyar to Iran, but as the revelry died down, she began to analyze the situation. After a lengthy visit to her parents' home, she came back with her revolutionary schedule considerably revised.

"Kamyar, much needs to be done in the U.S. It is not necessary for you to go back yet. Let's wait and see what happens," she said. The three of us were in a fast-food restaurant eating hamburgers. Kamyar slapped his hamburger down on the table. Ketchup went flying.

"Of course much needs to be done in the U.S. This is where it all starts. One can't even have a hamburger without fattening the pockets of corporations!"

"Kamyar," I said, "I haven't eaten all day. Let's have a cease-fire at least while we eat." This sent him into a tirade against imperialism. The end result was that he was hell-bent on going back and having his say.

"If you think they will let you just go around Iran gathering support for Communists, forget it," the new Carol said. "You haven't seen anything yet. You think enough people weren't killed during the

revolution—just wait and see. The real bloodbath is just starting."
They had argued this before. Carol had offered to marry Kamyar so
that he could stay in the U.S. as long as he wanted. Kamyar had said
that for all the laws are worth, such an arrangement was illegal.

Carol had pleaded with him, "It isn't illegal if you marry for
love." I was half-right and half-wrong about Carol. She would change
her politics, but not to protect her money. At this point she seemed
ready to register as a Republican if she thought it could save Kamyar's
life.

Marriage seemed like a good solution to me. They would take the
vows, Carol would abandon her claims to being a revolutionary, she
would get the stocks, and the two of them would go on a cruise to the
Caribbean, where Kamyar would have so much fun he would forget
about Imam Hossein and Jesus Christ. Carol's tender attentions would
slowly nurture Kamyar away from following his dead brother's foot-
steps and the two of them would live happily ever after.

But Kamyar, unmoved, left for Iran. I could not tell if Carol's
affection for him made his decision any harder. Despite my attempts
to bring up the subject, he had stuck to "real issues" in our conversations, and I suspect that the dialogues he held in his own head were
just as empty of personal concerns. As Carol had pointed out, his kind
of commitment is hard for me to visualize.

Carol and I were on our way back from the airport. I was driving
as Carol could not see for her tears. At the red light she burst out
crying anew.

"He didn't like to talk in the car except at red lights," she remembered.

"You sound like he is dead already. He'll probably get frustrated
and come back. Meanwhile, you can have a break from him. You
might even start laughing again."

"People said he didn't have a sense of humor, but he did. His
humor was just hard to understand," she said.

"Like what?" I was genuinely curious.

"Like when he borrowed my car without asking me. I freaked
out. I thought it had been stolen."

"That's funny?"

"No, wait. When he got back, I yelled at him for not leaving a note at least. He said he did leave a note. I said, 'Where did you leave it?' He said, 'Right on the windshield, plain as the nose on your face.'"

We drove quietly for a long time, not even talking at the red lights.

* * *

I found out about his death many years later. On the coffee table at a friend's house, a Farsi publication lay open. I flipped through it absently, finding only a crowded list of names with numbers in front of them.

"What's this, a phone book?" I started to say. Suddenly a jolt ran through my body. I almost dropped the book. Those were not phone numbers, they were execution dates. "Jesus Christ! This many?"

"Look through it," advised my host. "There is hardly anyone who can't find a name they recognize."

When I saw Kamyar's name on the list, I thought of Carol, I thought of his mother, and I thought of the pews with seat belts. Kamyar's comment about Christianity being a grand eulogy came to mind and brought a chuckle. I guess the boy did have a sense of humor. I wonder if they gave him any water before they shot him.

Epilogue

When our older daughter learned to read, I thought my evenings on the story couch would end. Sitting down, revered in many traditions as a resting posture, would no longer signal the invasion of mother bears, naughty rabbits, and clever maidens. But she figured out quickly that a story read silently is not the same as a story spoken out loud by the storyteller. The printed word remains more or less faithful to its author, while the spoken word derives its life from the sensations at hand and joins every here-and-now circus that happens along. So my restful evenings still make room for eyes pleading for stories that I have read over and over but never repeated.

The stories in this book will also be rendered by the circumstances under which they are told. As I write these words, the Middle East is in flames. Again. And worse than before. It is hard to tell how far the fire will spread this time or when it will subside. There is muscle flexing about the use of nuclear weapons, and I fear greatly for our world.

I wish I could say that an understanding of each other's cultures can help us settle our differences without destruction. But our armed conflicts rarely arise from misunderstandings. Those heartbreaking tragedies where the audience is tempted to jump on the stage and explain the mix-up to the actors are rare in the real world. The tragedy of war is a comedy in which the players bungle their lives with eyes wide open. No misunderstanding here, we fight to hang on to what we have or to get something we do not have. Reasons so pat it would take some alteration to garb them as misunderstandings.

The reward of contact with other cultures is spiritual. I found that out early in my friendship with a tree planter in Oregon. When I told him I was from Iran, he said he had never heard of that state. I told him Iran was not one of the fifty states, it was a separate country. He was astonished. Was that possible? I could see in his face even before I answered him that his mind was already racing far ahead of his questions. It was as though thousands of previously ignored obser-vations suddenly crystallized into one giant *of course*. This is the only unmistakable instance of revelation I have ever witnessed. Imagine his delight when I showed him that English was not the only language in the world.

Some friends do not believe me when I tell them this story. How could anyone not know that people are not the same all over? In a less extreme way, however, we are all awakened by contact with people who, for thousands of years, have taken a different path through the human mind. Just as variety of gene stock is hope for survival of a species during bad times, multiplicity of lifeviews keeps away despair when our established ways seem to fail us. The realization that the equation of life has infinite solutions inspires mind and spirit to continue searching. Who knows; on this pilgrimage we call evolu-tion, we may even find a way to rewrite our tragedies.

Today, with war a constant presence, I look at my stories in this way. But someday we will be at peace with all life on this planet. We will use our wealth to remedy inequalities and to give ourselves health-ier lives. We will apply our vast cunning to explore the universe that humbles us. Someday we will not waste our blessings in ignorance.

When that time comes, go to the attic, spank the dust off this book and tell these stories again. I am curious to hear their new meaning. If I am not here, my children will be.